# LOSING THE WILL

## J A Newman

**Jess** and **Eddie** welcome you to

**Bracken Farmhouse B&B and Self-Catering Barns.**

Situated at the end of a quiet lane in the heart of the Yorkshire Dales, **Bracken Farmhouse** is the perfect getaway holiday destination. The house dating from 1800 has four double rooms and one single, all with countryside views.

Also two newly converted self-catering barns **The Cow Shed** (sleeping 4) and **The Dog House** (sleeping 2) are situated in the landscaped grounds. Welcome pack on arrival.

Jessica's Parlour and tea garden, also open to non-residents, is the place to enjoy a hearty breakfast, a light lunch or one of Jess's many homemade cakes and bakes.

The village of Leadale has two pubs and the surrounding area is a haven for nature-lovers, walkers and cyclists.

Well-behaved dogs welcome.

Free Wi-Fi and private car park.

# LOSING THE WILL

## ONE

Jess's phone pinged. She quickly wiped her hands and read the text. 'Oh my God!'

'Wassup?' asked Eddie, dishing up two cooked breakfasts.

'The people staying in the Dog House have been delayed. That's all we need.'

'No sweat,' said Eddie, 'we'll sort it. Is Kate babysitting?'

Jess blew out a sigh. 'No, it's her birthday. Mike's taking her to the Red Lion.'

'What about Janie?'

Jess shrugged, put her phone down and took her loaded tray into Jessica's Parlour, the tearoom that doubled up as a dining room for her B&B guests. All the rooms were full and the tearoom hummed with cutlery on plates and happy chatter. When she opened Bracken Farmhouse she never dreamt she would be so busy. It was brilliant, of course, and Eddie helped, but she had been looking forward to the wedding reception tonight.

She pasted a smile on her face as she set the cooked breakfasts in front of two elderly ladies sitting by the window.

'That looks wonderful!' said one. 'Beautifully presented too.'

'Thanks,' said Jess. 'Can I get you anything else, more coffee? Toast?'

'More coffee would be lovely, thank you.'

Jess cleared a vacated table, pushed a couple of chairs in and took a tray of dirty pots back to the kitchen.

Eddie looked round from making a pot of tea. 'Head OK after last night?'

'I'm good thanks, Eddie. Can you take more coffee to table two while I take Eliot up for his nap?'

'Yeah, sure,' he said with a wink. 'I'll have a nice cappuccino waiting for you when you come down.'

Eliot started screaming. 'OK, OK, I'm on it.' Jess lifted her baby out of the highchair and took him upstairs.

Eddie dealt with the coffees and made sure the other guests were happy then set about making Jess's cappuccino and loading the dishwasher. He was hoping to escape to his workshop this morning. They were raking it in but he was worried that Jess was overdoing it; what with the B&B, the morning coffee, lunches and afternoon teas, and eight-month-old Eliot. It was all getting a bit much. Eddie had suggested they employ some more staff but Jess wasn't having any of it. Right from the start she had decided to do everything herself including all her own baking. He helped as much as possible, of course, as he'd promised right at the beginning, but every night Jess was so tired she was asleep as soon as her head touched the pillow.

Jess came back and Eddie set the cappuccino in front of her. 'Here, sit down, take five.'

'I can't, not yet.' There was a customer waiting by the till with a bag of homemade choc-chip cookies in his hand.

'I'll go,' said Eddie, but she was already there. She took their money, cleared two more tables and came back to find she was on her own.


Mandy stretched lazily and remembered last night. She had been surprised that Jess and Eddie had managed to get the Cow Shed and the Dog House up and running for the start of the season. They'd thought of everything including standard bay trees in pots by the doors and window boxes full of brightly coloured petunias. Stepping inside the Cow Shed the scent of new wood had greeted her. 'Gosh, Jess! It's fab. I love it!'

Jess, complete with Eliot on hip, had accompanied Mandy and her eight-year-old twin girls, Kirsty and Keira, who immediately ran off to find out where they were sleeping.

Mandy's husband Trevor had grinned at Eddie, 'Looks cool, mate. And the little one next door.'

'Yeah,' said Eddie, 'the Dog House. Go and have a look. It's open.'

'Well,' said Mandy, inspecting the fitted kitchen and the seating areas in the Cow Shed, 'you'd never guess this was just a pile of rubble last year.'

Jess smiled smugly and moved Eliot to her other hip. 'Thanks, it's all been a bit crazy but I'm pleased with them.'

Eliot started wriggling and pulling Jess's hair.

'Aw,' said Mandy, 'give him to me. He's gorgeous. But I don't know how you manage, what with the business and everything.' She hugged the baby and planted a kiss on his cheek.

'Yeah, tell me about it!' Jess pushed a strand of hair behind her ear and smoothed down her top. 'Anyway, all set for Monika's wedding tomorrow?'

'Yeah, I'm really looking forward to it.'

'So am I, but we won't be able to get there till the evening.'

'That's a shame. It's all set to be one hell-of-a-do. Thornwood Manor looks stunning on the website.'

'Yeah, it's cool, although I've only ever been past it.'

Kirsty and Keira had come running in with a basket of decorated cookies. 'Look what we've got!' said Kirsty.

'And we've got our own bathroom!' said Keira, jumping up and down.

Yes, thought Mandy, Jess had thought of everything including the delicious meal in the farmhouse kitchen last night. But Mandy was now regretting that she'd drunk so much. She sat up and swallowed two pain-killers. Checked the time on her phone and snuggled back up to Trevor.

Meanwhile, the twins had got up and dressed and sneaked out to do some exploring. A little way along the road they'd found two donkeys in a field. One of them plodded over to the fence braying loudly. It was a bit scary but he seemed friendly enough so Kirsty began to stroke the soft oily fur between his ears. Keira hung back at first but when she saw there was nothing to worry about she did the same.

Kirsty looked across the field and pointed. 'Look, caravans!'

'So?' .

'I bet they're gypsies.'

'Don't you mean travellers?'

'Well, Enid Blyton calls them gypsies. It's in that book at Grandma's, *Five Go to Mystery Moor*, remember? Come on, let's go see.'

Keira frowned and stuck out her bottom lip. 'I don't want to. I'm going back.'

'Oh, come on, don't be such a wuss.' Kirsty ducked through the ranch fence and started across the boggy field.

'Ugh, I don't like it,' moaned Keira, her shoes sinking into the ground.

Kirsty ignored her, hid behind a bush and lowered her voice. 'Look, we'll just spy on them for a bit.'

Keira looked in the direction of the Cow Shed. 'But Mum and Dad will be wondering where we are. And I'm hungry.'

'Stop whinging, I just want to see who lives there.'

'No one, probably, those caravans are all green and slimy.'

Just then, a woman jumped down from one of the caravans, her long unkempt hair pushed behind her ears. Her multi-coloured skirt swished against her muddy boots as she began making her way over to a standpipe carrying a big plastic bucket.

'Told you,' hissed Kirsty, 'gypsies!'

'Well, I don't like it. What if they kidnap us? I'm going back.' Keira turned and began to pick her way over the uneven ground while Kirsty continued to spy on the woman.

'There you are!' shouted Mandy running up to the fence. 'I've been looking everywhere. Oh my God, look at the state of you! What were you thinking? Come on, we'll never get to Monika's wedding at this rate.'

She helped her daughters over the fence and took them back to the Cow Shed; the twins' shoes leaving a mud trail on the path.

'Take 'em off,' said Mandy, when they reached the Cow Shed. 'I don't want you dropping mud all over Jess's floor.'

Trevor stifled a giggle as Mandy held Kirsty's shoes aloft.

'It's not funny, they both need hosing down and we're running late! State of 'em and that's the only pair of shoes she's got. Keira's are just as bad. I wish we hadn't forgotten their wedding shoes.'

'Give 'em here,' said Trevor. 'I saw a tap outside.'

'Thanks, love.'

Trevor sauntered across the lawn to Eddie's workshop where he'd seen the outside tap and proceeded to remove what mud he could from both pairs of shoes.

Eddie opened the workshop door. 'All right there, mate?'

Trevor held up the dripping shoes. 'Yeah, I've rinsed 'em off. I just need a cloth.'

Eddie laughed. 'Kids, eh?' He pulled out a clean cloth from one of the drawers in the workbench and handed it to Trevor.

Trevor turned to look out the window. 'I envy you, living the dream here in the Dales.'

'Yeah, it's great but it's a lot of work.'

'To be honest,' said Trevor, rubbing vigorously at the shoes, 'I'm getting fed up of being a superstore manager, staff problems, stroppy customers, stock not arriving on time. Sometimes I feel like jacking it all in.'

Eddie's eyebrows shot up, 'Really? What else would you do?'

Trevor shrugged.

'What does Mandy think?'

'I dunno, I haven't told her, but I fancy slowing down a pace, taking things a bit easier, you know?'

'Escape to the country, you mean?' Eddie smiled.

'Huh, yeah, somethin' like that.'

'Well, I can recommend it. Like I said, this place is a lot of work but I'm glad we took the plunge, or rather Jess did. It's a world away from Peckham.' Eddie still couldn't believe his luck when he thought about it. Two years ago, after Jess's sister Shelley had delved into their family history, they had both unexpectedly come into an inheritance. But Eddie hadn't thought he stood a chance of sharing it with Jess, not when she'd been hooked up with that posh lawyer bloke Giles Morgan. But Eddie had played it cool and, in the end, Jess had come round to his way of thinking, that they were two peas in the same pod.

Trevor put the cloth back on the bench and scrutinised the shoes. 'I guess they'll have to do.'

'They're fine. Listen, any time you wanna chat?'

'Thanks mate. Anyway, best get back before Mandy has a meltdown.'


Two hours later, Mandy straightened Trevor's purple tie and brushed a piece of lint from his jacket, 'Mm, very smart.' She planted a smacker on his cheek, wiped off the smear of lipstick and gave the twins the once-over. 'Turn round.' She scrutinised their electric blue bridesmaids' dresses that complimented their nut-brown skin and their tight shoe-string plaits. 'OK, your shoes will have to do.'

Trevor winked at his daughters. 'You look awesome!' They grinned at him.

'How do I look?' asked Mandy, doing a twirl in her close-fitting fuchsia-pink dress, heels to match, all topped off with a feathery fascinator.

Trevor pulled her into his arms.

'Here, steady on! It took me ages to get this silly thing to go right.' She turned back to the mirror and fixed the creation with another hairgrip. 'Right, let's go!'

Jess ran out and stopped them at the gate. 'Hey! Let me look.'

Mandy and the girls stood in a line and did a twirl.

'Oh wow! You all look awesome. Have a lovely time.'

'Thanks Jess. We've got a lovely day for it,' said Mandy, blinking up at the cloudless sky. 'See you later.'

As the twins sat in the back seat, Kirsty saw the woman they'd seen coming out of the caravan earlier. She nudged her sister. They both watched silently as the woman made her way towards the back door of Bracken Farmhouse.

Trevor drove them smoothly out of the car park as another car drove in. 'Looks like Jess is in for another busy day.'

'Yeah, it's fantastic,' said Mandy. 'The place is buzzing.'

In the kitchen, Jess wiped her brow and turned to see her neighbour entering the back door. 'There you are, Janie. I was starting to think you weren't coming. You all right?'

The woman nodded.

'Most of the B&Bs have checked out but I could do with a hand in here.'

'Aye, what d'you want me to do, then?'

'Well, scrub your hands and stick an apron on for a start. And tie your hair up. I'll get done if health and safety see you like that.'

Janie headed for the utility room while Jess loaded two plates with jacket potatoes and salad and took them into Jessica's Parlour, shouting over her shoulder, 'You can get the next batch of scones out, if you like?'

Janie found the oven cloth and took the tray of fruit scones out of the Aga. Trying not to burn her fingers as she placed them one by one on the wire rack, she breathed in the delicious smell. She was tempted to pinch one. She'd had nothing to eat since last night's beans on toast.

A heavy sigh escaped Jess as she dumped another tray of dirty dishes on the worktop.

Janie looked at her. 'I reckon you could do with some more help, Jess.'

'We're fine at the minute. You still OK for tonight, though?'

Janie wrinkled her nose. 'I hope so. Neptune's off his food. I don't like t' look of him to be honest. I had to call t' vet this morning but he can't come till five.'

Jess's heart sank. She'd been looking forward to this wedding reception at Thornwood Manor for months.

Eddie came sauntering in. 'All right, Janie?'

She nodded, 'Just been tellin' Jess – one of me donkey's is ailin'. I need to be home by four-thirty.'

Eddie glanced at Jess pouring hot soup into bowls. 'Here, Janie, stick your head round the door and see if anyone wants to order, would you?'

'Sure.' Janie smoothed her apron and took out her pad and pen.

'And take these with you,' said Jess. 'Table four.'

Jess checked the orders pinned to the dresser. She was having a job to keep up. 'One carrot and coriander soup with wholemeal bread, two jackets with tuna mayo, one cheese melt, two teas and a cappuccino. Oh, and jug of iced water.'

Eddie quickly scrubbed his hands, attended to the drinks and reloaded the dishwasher. After what Trevor had told him there was a seed of an idea beginning to grow in his mind.

# TWO

Jess checked her phone for the umpteenth time. No messages. Where the hell were Mr and Mrs Dean? It was getting late and she'd heard nothing from Janie either. Jess felt like Cinderella. If only she had a fairy godmother.

Eddie breezed in from the workshop and saw Jess scrolling through her phone. She shook her head. 'Still no word from the guests staying in the Dog House.'

'You well-named it, then!'

Jess gave him one of her looks. She wasn't amused.

'What about Janie?'

'Nope, still nothing from her.'

'Look, it's not the end of the world. We can take Eliot with us. It's not a problem.'

'If Janie doesn't turn up we won't be going at all.' She chucked her phone on the table.

Eddie turned her to face him. 'Hey, we'll get there, OK?' He planted a slow sensuous kiss on her lips just as the house phone shrilled. She pounced on it. 'Hello, Bracken Farmhouse.' Jess heard some bickering on the other end then a woman's voice.

'Oh hi, sorry, we're staying in the Dog House, Mr and Mrs Dean, but we can't find you. The sat nav's taken us all down the lanes.'

'OK, where are you?'

'That's just it, we haven't a clue.'

Jess blew out her cheeks, 'Did you pass the Green Man?'

'I think so.'

'Right, get back there and take the first on the left. Follow the road round and you'll find us at the end of the drive, OK? Got that?'

'I think so. Thanks.'

'Good. We'll see you soon.'

Eddie watched Jess scrolling through her phone again. 'Well?'

'They've got lost and there's still nothing from Janie.'

He glanced at the kitchen clock. 'Look, there's still time. Go and have a soak in the tub, I'll look after things here.'

Jess threw her arms round Eddie's neck and hugged him. 'Thanks love. I'm sorry I'm a bit snappy, it's just…'

Eddie silenced her with a kiss, ran his hands down her back and gave her bottom a squeeze. 'Mm, let's not get carried away or we'll *never* get there! Go on, I'll come up and scrub your back in a tic.'

Jess couldn't resist checking on Eliot in the purple and lemon nursery. He looked so peaceful asleep in his cot with his thumb in his mouth. It would be such a shame to wake him to take him to the reception. Jess wondered if Janie would turn up and if she should leave Eliot with her. She didn't think Janie was used to babies. Jess had a sudden rush of love for her son. He was all so perfect, wisps of blond hair curling onto his forehead. When she'd held him for the first time she had worried about the unfamiliar task of motherhood ahead of her but Eddie had made light of it, 'Ha, yeah, you get more instructions with a microwave!' Eight months. Where had that time gone? Oh my God! Time! She hurried to the bathroom, turned on the taps and added her favourite Givenchy foam bath.

Downstairs, Janie barged in through the back door with her hair all over the place.

'I'm really sorry Eddie. The vet were late.' She looked around. 'Where's Jess?'

'Getting ready. Look Janie, if it's too much trouble…'

She shook her head, 'No, no, it's fine and anyway, what else would I be doing?'

Eddie felt a bit sorry for Janie, living on her own in a bug-hutch of a cottage with only her cat for company and now one of her donkeys was probably on his way to the great paddock in the sky. 'How's Neptune?'

Janie took a deep breath and chewed her lip, 'Doesn't look good. If he doesn't improve in the next few days…' she shrugged. 'The vet thinks it could be COPD, maybe from mouldy hay. That means Pluto might go same way.'

Eddie didn't know what to say. He knew nothing about donkeys but he thought she could do with a drink to cheer her up, 'Cup o' tea, glass of wine?'

'I'd love a glass of wine but I think I'd better stick to tea, thanks Eddie. I need to keep me wits about me tonight.'

Eddie went to put the kettle on then realised he needed to get moving himself. 'All right if I leave you to it?'

Janie nodded and cast her eyes over the kitchen. It was hard to believe the place had been a hive of activity a few hours ago. There wasn't a crumb in sight and all the work surfaces were gleaming. She had to hand it to Jess.

Meanwhile Mr and Mrs Dean had finally found their way to Bracken Farmhouse and screeched to a halt in the car park. Mr Dean slammed the car door, strode up to the farmhouse and banged loudly on the door. After a few seconds it opened a crack.

'Hello?'

He glared at Janie, 'Mr and Mrs Dean?' When there was no response he spat, 'We've booked, to stay in the Dog House!'

'Oh, er… if you'd like to wait in here…I'll go and fetch the key.' She shot off down the hallway.

'I told you we shouldn't have booked this place,' snapped Mr Dean. 'Huh, the Dog House. I only hope it doesn't smell of dog! And they need to do something about that bloody awful approach road.'

His wife was near to tears. She'd had enough. The journey had been a trial and now it looked as though they might have to find another place for the night.

Janie came back empty-handed. 'Sorry, if you'll just bear with. Be back in a tic.'

Mr Dean huffed, walked a few paces down the hall and glimpsed Jessica's Parlour through the open door – crisp white tablecloths, spotless flagstones. 'Well, at least that looks up to the mark; can't say as much for the owner.'

His wife scowled at him. 'God's sake, Roger. Lighten up. This is meant to be fun.'

Janie came back at last merrily waving the key. 'Here we are, then, if you'd like to follow me.' She led them out the front door, down the side of the house, past the conservatory and across the back lawn. Mrs Dean looked all around while her husband stared straight ahead.

Opening the door to the Dog House, Janie stood back and glanced at the sumptuous furnishings and the welcome pack on the kitchen counter. It could've fed her for a week. 'Aye, I'm sure you'll be very cosy. Enjoy!'

# THREE

Jess hummed to herself as she worked. In the end she'd had a wonderful evening at the wedding buffet with Eddie, Mandy and Trevor and the twins. Mandy's cousin had looked stunning in her ivory bridal gown and Jess wondered if she'd ever get the chance to marry Eddie or if they could afford such a lavish do. Over-the-top pink flower arrangements were everywhere, the food and wine had flowed, and the live band had played *Material Girl.* What was there not to like? Of course, this had made Jess think of Shelley, her older wayward sister who had introduced her to Madonna. She hadn't seen or heard from her since she'd departed with Giles in his yacht for the French coast. That was two years ago. A few months later Giles had returned without Shelley – she had got hooked up with a bunch of Aussies and gone on another adventure. Jess got to wondering where Shelley was now and what she was doing with her life.

Heavy footsteps on the gravel and a bang on the kitchen door brought Jess out of her daydream.

'Oh hi,' realising it must be Mr Dean who had spent the night in the Dog House with his wife, she asked, 'everything all right?'

'Finally,' he grumped. 'Who are you? Where's the owner of this place?'

'I *am* the owner. Sorry I wasn't here to greet you last night but we…'

'…in that case, you need to choose your staff more carefully.' He shoved the key at Jess and turned to his wife. 'Got everything? Right, let's be off.'

Mrs Dean pulled a face and lowered her voice. 'Take no notice of Roger. I think you're doing a wonderful job. I would've asked you if we could stay longer but we're touring. Next stop, the lakes.'

Jess felt like saying good luck but bit her tongue, 'How lovely. Glad you enjoyed it. Maybe we'll see you again?'

'Oh, I do hope so.'

No sooner had Jess closed the door than the twins burst in wearing jeans and tee shirts and broad grins.

'Hi,' said Jess. 'Had your breakfast?'

They looked at each other and shook their heads.

Jess decided to play a little game with them. She put on her posh voice. 'In that case ladies, perhaps you'd like to take a seat in the parlour? You'll find a menu on the table.'

Keira was unsure but Kirsty played along with it and pulled her sister to the table set for two. They sat opposite each other and began to look at their menus.

Jess stood poised with pad and pen. 'What can I get you?'

They were taking a while to decide so Jess went back to the kitchen to ring Mandy. She lowered her voice. 'Hi, the twins are in here, I'm giving 'em breakfast.'

'Aw, you sure? You've got enough to do.'

'It's fine. I thought I'd give 'em a little treat.'

'We're not up yet, anyway.'

'Cool, take your time. They're all right in here.'

'Thanks Jess.'

'Hey, before you go, did you see that couple staying in the Dog House?'

'No, why?'

'Well, the husband was a right grumpy sod. He shoved the key in my hand and said I should choose my staff more carefully. Bloody cheek! I know Janie's a bit slow but…'

'…I shouldn't worry. You're doing fine.'

'Well I hope he doesn't leave me a bad review.' Jess heard the rustle of sheets. She couldn't remember the last time she and Eddie had had a lie-in.

She went back to find the twins patiently waiting, menus in hand. They gave her their order and she promptly returned with two plates of sausages, baked beans and hash browns. 'Anything to drink?'

'Orange juice, please,' they chorused.

Jess poured two glasses of the freshly squeezed juice and set them down. 'Enjoy!'

'This looks yummy!' said Kirsty.

'Thank you, Auntie Jess,' said Keira.

Bless 'em, she thought, they hadn't called her Auntie for ages, but then again, they were growing up and probably thought it was uncool. She began rearranging the goods for sale on the dresser and generally tidying up.

Kirsty looked up, 'Auntie Jess, who owns those donkeys in the field?'

'Ah, that's Janie.'

'Is she a gypsy?'

Jess chuckled and shook her head. 'No, she's the lady who comes in to help me sometimes.'

'What are the donkey's names?' asked Keira.

'Neptune and Pluto.'

'Oh, like the planets. We've been doing that at school,' said Keira. 'Neptune and Pluto are the furthest away from the sun.'

Jess ruminated on this fascinating fact. She couldn't remember learning stuff like that at her school.

'Can we have a ride on them?' asked Kirsty, 'you know, like on the beach.'

'You'll have to ask Janie but I doubt it. '

The twins both screwed up their noses. 'Why not?' asked Kirsty.

'They're retired.'

'Oh, like Grandma!'

Jess smiled to herself.

*

Eddie and Trevor entered The Green Man to the fug of Sunday lunch.

'What you having, Trev?'

'I'll get these.'

'No, my shout.'

'Thanks mate.' Trevor nodded to the real ale. 'Better make it half. I've gotta drive home later.'

Eddie waved a ten-pound note in the barman's direction. 'A pint and a half of your best, please Greg.'

Trevor watched him swish his dreadlocks behind his shoulders as he pulled the pint. Two men were propping up the bar at the other end but apart from them the place was full of people enjoying a roast dinner; it was making him hungry. He nodded appreciatively at the décor, taking it all in. Oriental wood carvings, Indian fabrics and Pagan symbols. 'Cool.'

Greg handed Trevor his half. 'You wanna look at a menu? Specials on da board.'

'Cheers mate,' said Eddie. 'Another time. Jess is cooking.'

'How is Jess and the little one?'

'All good, thanks, mate. Catch you later.'

They sat at a table with a carved green man staring at them from the opposite wall. Eddie noticed Trevor looking around. 'Yeah, I like it in here. The Red Lion's full of toffs and this is staggering distance. Not that I do much staggering these days.'

'So, you don't come in here much, then?'

'No, not anymore but Greg's a good guy, knows his stuff. He had a few hiccups at first, you know, getting accepted by some of the old locals and stuff, but it's all good now.'

'Where's he from?'

Eddie shrugged. 'Somewhere in London, Brixton I think. History's a bit like yours. He's got a wife and a couple o' kids. She does most of the cooking.'

Trevor nodded. He'd noticed a few eyes on him when he came in. He sipped his ale and smacked his lips. 'Mm, I could get used to this.'

Eddie smiled. 'I've been thinking…you know what you said on Friday night?'

'What? About chucking ma job in?'

'Yeah, you serious?'

'Could be…I dunno, it's when I come up here, the pace of life and the countryside…'

'So, why don't you?'

Trevor fixed his dark brown eyes on Eddie. 'Nothing I'd like more but there's a lot to think about.' He took another mouthful of ale. 'Maybe in the future.'

'Yeah, but you should do it now, while you're still young enough. And if you really hate your job…' Eddie smiled at the thought. 'I know Jess would be over the moon to have you and Mandy up here.'

Trevor grinned showing his perfect teeth.

'And your kids would love it too. I only wish I'd done it years ago.' He took a swig of ale. 'I would've have done if Jess had been willing. I kept suggesting it but she poo-pooed it. It was only her trip to Yorkshire with that Giles bloke that changed her mind.'

Trevor nodded. His mind was racing – put the house on the market, find a house in the Dales. Maybe a job transfer…but would Mandy want to leave her mum in Peckham and what about her job? Then there were Kirsty and Keira to think about. Would they want to leave Grandma and be uprooted from their school and their friends? But he didn't think his parents would mind;

they were all for them getting ahead. 'Yeah, there's a lot to think about.'

Eddie remembered Mandy and Trevor's three-bed semi on Peckham Rye. 'You'd have no trouble selling your house. You're only twenty minutes from the city and it must be worth a few bob by now.' He waited, hoping he wasn't pushing too hard.

Trevor drained his glass, put it down and rolled it between his big brown hands. 'It's a nice thought. I'd have to talk it over with Mandy of course, do a few sums, get the house valued.' But the excitement was starting to show in his eyes.

Eddie beamed and gave him a playful punch.


Jess and Mandy had laughed their way through a bottle of pinot grigio and were now on their second. Jess had mashed some of the vegetables with gravy for Eliot and the twins had fed him in his highchair. All the excitement had worn him out and he was now asleep in his cot.

Eddie and Trevor burst in arm in arm.

'Oh, hello,' said Jess, 'and what've you two been cookin' up?'

'Nothing as good as you girls,' said Eddie, sniffing the air.

Mandy put a saucepan in the sink and turned to Trevor. 'OK, so what's happening?'

'Nothin' much.'

'Yeah, right.'

'I'm starving,' said Trevor, trying to change the subject.

Jess watched Eddie and Trevor. They looked like a couple of naughty children who had been caught doing something they shouldn't.

The twins sat eagerly waiting for their dinner while Jess carved the succulent leg of lamb roasted to perfection, the sprigs of rosemary turned brown and crisp. She held out a piece of meat to each of them on her carving fork. They blew on it, popped it in and chewed hungrily.

'Honestly,' said Mandy, 'anyone would think you hadn't been fed for a month.'

The plates of meat, puffy Yorkshire puddings and crispy roast potatoes were passed around the table, dishes of vegetables and lastly the gravy boat centre stage. Mandy dished up some food for the twins and poured on some of Jess's rich gravy. They couldn't wait any longer and began shovelling the food into their mouths.

'Oi,' said Mandy, 'where's your manners?' They put their knives and forks down. 'You know not to start before everyone else.'

'Right,' said Jess, sitting down, 'now we're all sorted, what you got to tell us?'

# FOUR

Jess snuggled up to Eddie and slowly remembered it was Monday, baking day. Although she loved and took pride in her work, keeping all the balls in the air was exhausting, but maybe if Mandy and Trevor moved up here it would take some of the pressure off.

After their Sunday lunch they had all taken their drinks out to the sun-soaked garden with endless views of drystone walls and undulating countryside. Eddie had been right; she was over the moon at the thought of having Mandy on the doorstep again and Mandy had relished the thought of starting a new life in the Dales but she wasn't looking forward to telling her mum that they were thinking of moving hundreds of miles away. Mandy and Trevor had lived close to Carol ever since they'd got married and she loved having the twins but this seemed the only sticking point. Jess hoped that they were serious about the move.

Baby noises were filtering through from the nursery. Aware of every little sound, Jess bounced out of bed and padded across the landing. Drawing back the curtains she found Eliot chuckling as he pulled himself up on the cot bars. He was growing fast. He'd soon be crawling then walking and getting into mischief. She picked him up and brushed his blond curls off his clammy forehead, changed his nappy and took him downstairs for his breakfast.

She'd just made Eliot's porridge when Janie burst in looking more dishevelled than ever. On closer inspection Jess could see she'd been crying, 'Oh my God, Janie. What is it?'

Janie dragged a hand through her hair and hung her head. 'It's Neptune. He's worse, I think I'll have to phone t' vet. Oh Jess,' her face crumpled, 'I don't want him to lose him but I don't want him to suffer.'

Jess put down Eliot's porridge and gave her a hug. 'Maybe it won't come to that. Come and sit down. I'll make some tea.'

Eliot began banging his tray and making impatient noises.

'I'll make a brew,' said Janie, 'you carry on.'

'He should really be feeding himself but I can't stand the mess.'

There was a knock on the back door. 'Bright's Laundry,' shouted the woman and dumped a heavy parcel inside the door. 'All right, love? Got some for me to take back?'

Jess pointed to the other bundle on the floor.

'Ta, love. See yer next week,' she lifted the bundle onto her trolley and trundled back to the van. That one drove off and another took its place. A woman with a stack of eggs came in and left them on the little table.

'Thanks, Mabel. Settle up next week, OK?'

Last but not least was Sam who came in with a box of assorted breads. He left it by the utility room and sat down on the chair by the door.

'Thanks Sam. Tea?'

He nodded, 'Thanks lass. Yours is me last call so there's no hurry.'

'Bye 'eck, Jess,' said Janie, 'you're all go. I don't know how you do it.'

'I'm fine, Eddie'll be down in a minute.' She poked the last spoonful of porridge into Eliot's open mouth and carefully scraped the excess off his sore chin.

'He's a bonny lad is that one,' said Sam, watching Jess lowering Eliot into his walker, 'takes after his da.'

Jess smiled. Sam was one of the real old locals whose great grandfather had started the village bakery before the war. It had been passed down to Sam and then to his son who was now in charge. The bakery, like other businesses in the area, due to the upsurge in tourism and holiday homes, was now enjoying an increase in sales and Sam had been brought back out of retirement to help with the deliveries.

Janie set three mugs of tea on the table. Sam got up and stirred two sugars into his and sat back down cradling the mug in his lap, quietly observing.

Janie stared into her mug. 'I'll go when I've had this. I don't wanna put on yer. It's just…'

Jess shook her head, 'You're fine, Janie. You know we're always here for you.' She wiped Eliot's highchair down and pushed it to one side.

The phone shrilled.

'Shall I get it?' asked Janie.

'No, it'll go onto answerphone in a bit,' said Jess.

A man's voice cut in on the phone, 'Er, Mr Gilbert? Mr Fairview here. Thanks for getting in touch...appreciated. I really wanted to speak to you but I'll try again later... cheers.'

Jess frowned. It didn't sound like a booking.

Eddie breezed in, his fair hair wet from the shower, 'Hi, Janie, Sam. All right?'

They both nodded.

'How's the van going now, Sam? All right is it?'

'It's running lovely, lad. You've got the magic touch, you have that.'

Eddie beamed and said to Jess, 'I'll check the laundry later. Let's hope it's all here this time.'

'A Mr Fairview just left a message on the answerphone,' said Jess, watching for Eddie's reaction.

He raised his eyebrows and shrugged, 'And?'

'Said he really wanted to speak to you but he'll try again later.'

'Oh, right.' Eddie took out the pans and baking trays. 'You staying for breakfast, Janie? What about you, Sam?'

'No thanks lad,' said Sam, placing his empty mug on the table. 'I'll be off now. Thanks for me tea.'

Janie stood up. 'I should be off, too.'

'Go on, Janie,' said Eddie, 'a good old fry-up will do you world o' good.' He always thought she looked half-starved and it might go some way towards cheering her up.

She smiled shyly. 'Well, if you don't mind...' she sat down again, 'but I ought to be helping yer instead of sitting here like Lady Muck.' She looked from one to the other. 'You're always slavin' away, the pair of yer, and there's me...'

'Actually,' said Jess, 'do you think you could check the laundry? It's heavy so Eddie will take it through to the conservatory for you. There's an itemised sheet – it's quite easy.'

'Sure.'

'So,' started Jess, when Janie was safely out of earshot and Eddie was back in the kitchen, 'what you got to tell me?'

'About what?'

'Come on, *Mr Gilbert.*'

The footfall on the stairs told Eddie the guests were about to take their places in the tearoom. 'I need to start cooking and you need to get dressed!'

'All right, but you're not gettin' away with it that easily!' Jess threw the tea towel at him. He caught it and grinned.

In the conservatory Janie opened the parcel of laundry and breathed in the clean fresh scent. Tentatively stroking one of the pure white towels against her cheek, she remembered when she used to help her mam fold up her little brother's nappies fresh off the line. She could still remember his little face looking up at her and how he felt when she cuddled him. She pushed the memory away and began to check all the bed linen and towels against the list. Thankfully it was all in order. Her task completed she was drawn back to the kitchen by the delicious aromas.

'All done.'

'Thanks Janie.' Eddie set two plates of cooked breakfast on a tray. 'That's for table two.'

Jess came in and whisked the tray away. She didn't want her guests subjected to Janie's appearance this morning. If Janie was going to help in the tearoom on a regular basis, she would have to have a quiet word with her.

'What'll it be then, Janie?' asked Eddie, loading up a plate. He didn't wait for an answer. He piled the food up and placed it in front of her. 'There you go.' Janie stared at her plate. 'Not veggie are you?' Janie shook her head. 'Good. Sauce in the sachets and bread's next to the toaster. Help yourself.'

In all the kerfuffle they'd forgotten about Eliot who was now making angry noises, his walker stuck against the sofa at the other end of the kitchen.

'You need L plates, lad!' said Janie. His little face lit up and her heart melted. Jess rushed in and unhooked him.

'Anyway,' said Janie, putting her knife and fork together, 'I'll be off now, unless you need me to help with washin' up?'

'No, you're OK,' said Jess. 'Let me know what happens with Neptune, though.'

'Will do.'

As soon as she'd gone, Jess turned to Eddie. 'Right, let's have it.'

'What?'

'Mr Fairview?'

'Oh right.' He looked cagily at her. 'I did mention it before but I don't think you were listening. I want to get into vintage cars, as a business.' He took the tea towel from her, put it down and turned her to face him. 'I've worked it all out. Got the room, the workshop and it's working on cars again, what I know best. Don't look at me like that. I'll still help you in here.'

'Oh my God Eddie, we're stretched as it is.'

'We'll advertise for more help.'

She shook her head. 'We can't afford it, you know that.'

'Don't worry, we'll work it out. I won't get many at first, anyway. It's just something I gotta do, OK?'

The woman who came in to do the change-overs arrived.

'Hi Kate.' Jess gave her the key to the Dog House. 'I haven't been in there so I don't know how they've left it.'

'No problem. Is it just that one today, then?'

'Yep, but I might have to rethink these one-nighters.'

'Well, if you don't mind me saying, you are looking a bit tired lately, Jess. What with the baby and the baking and everything. Perhaps you need some more help?'

Jess was immediately on the defensive. 'I can handle it and Eddie helps…'

Kate lifted her eyebrows, waiting for more.

'Yeah, it's just…sometimes…oh, I dunno but it would be nice to get out and make friends, take Eliot to toddlers, stuff like that. One day.'

'Babies grow up fast you know – before you know it, they're off to school and then leaving home. Anyway, I'll make a start.' She went to pick up the clean bed linen then hesitated. 'I noticed your lawns need cutting. Shall I tell Mike? He's got time this afternoon...'

'Thanks Kate but Eddie's doing it later.'

'Sure?'

'Quite sure.' Jess almost pushed her out the door. Huh! Telling her when her grass needed cutting! Bloody cheek! But Kate was right about one thing. Jess didn't want to turn round one day and realise she'd missed out on Eliot's development but, on the other hand, she'd put so much of herself into her business she couldn't imagine leaving it to anyone else.

In the Dog House Kate set to work stripping the bed and remaking it. She scrubbed and polished and flew around with the vacuum cleaner. It wasn't too bad; the guests had only stayed one night, but her pride dictated she left it spotless. Standing back to appraise her work a big smile settled on her face. Yeah, she was good. Too good for Bracken Farmhouse and the money Jess was paying her! She opened the fridge to remove any food that might've been left and spied a ready-meal of duck with cherry sauce and a fancy dessert, checked they were still in date and popped them in her bag. That was tonight's dinner sorted. Just enough time to check the bathroom, the lounge area and lastly the bedroom to see if the guests had left anything else behind. As she opened the top drawer in the bedside table something rolled forward. It looked like a gold ring. On closer inspection she realised it was a wedding ring. She tried it for size but it wouldn't go on any of her fat fingers. It would fetch a pretty penny on eBay but that was very dishonest of her. No, on second thoughts, she popped it in her jeans pocket and made a mental note to give it to Jess.

# FIVE

Mandy was enjoying a breather after a busy day at Top to Toe. The twins had been invited to tea at a friend's house on this warm sunny evening and she was making the most of a couple of hours to herself pottering in the garden.

Jess had recommended that Mandy and Trevor ask Jenkins & Co estate agents for a valuation on their house at Peckham Rye. Mandy had rung in her lunch hour and Chris Jenkins had said he was more than happy to oblige, in fact he had a slot this evening if it was convenient. Mandy had jumped at the chance. Whilst at work today it had hit her that, apart from Liz, the owner of Top to Toe who had been there for decades, Mandy was the longest serving member of the beauty salon. She and Jess used to have a laugh with Silvana, Connie and Sarah, not only in the salon but nights out at Saucy Meg's ale house, but they had all moved on within the last two years and Mandy felt left behind. She didn't have anything in common with the younger beauty therapists with their pumped-up lips and clown eyebrows or the hairstylists who were always talking about their conquests. The more she thought about it, the more she couldn't wait to hand in her notice. Also, being with Jess and Eddie again had reinforced how much she missed Jess and how chilled-out she and Trevor always felt in the Dales.

Donning her gardening gloves to protect her manicure she set to work pulling out the dandelions that had shot up while her back was turned. She enjoyed whiling away a few hours, digging and planting, letting her mind drift. It was therapy. Owing to the kitchen extension, the back garden had been reduced to a minimum but there was always something to do. She turned to see the yellow climbing rose had made another bid for freedom and she set to work tying in the new shoots.

Trevor shouted from the patio doors. 'All right, love? I got off early.'

Mandy threw her gloves and fork down and ran to kiss him. 'Good timing!'

'Oh, why's that?'

'The twins are at Sky's for tea and Chris Jenkins is coming to value the house in an hour.' She went to the fridge and poured two glasses of sauvignon blanc and handed one to Trevor. 'Didn't you get my message?'

'Been too busy. You didn't waste any time.'

'Well, why put it off if?'

'Oh, don't get me wrong, it's just…I thought you'd wanna run it past your mum first.'

'It's only a valuation.'

Trevor nodded. 'True.' He loosened the collar of his polo shirt and drank deeply. 'Mm, I needed that.'

'Bad day?'

He screwed up his nose. 'Nothing out the ordinary. I've been thinking…I could ask for a transfer to one of the smaller stores in the Dales, rather than looking for a different kind of job. It might not be as demanding as managing a huge superstore.'

'Maybe you should ask about that before we put the house on the market? Have you said anything about leaving?'

'Not yet. Have you?'

Mandy shook her head. 'Let's see what Chris Jenkins has to say first.' The doorbell rang. 'Talking of which…'

Chris Jenkins stood in the porch adjusting his tie and his glasses. He'd had a quick look around outside and was looking forward to having this property on his books.

'Mrs King?' He shook her hand. 'Good evening, Chris Jenkins. I hope I'm not too early?'

'No, not at all, come through.' Mandy led him into the immaculate open-plan kitchen where Trevor sat at the breakfast bar.

'Ah, Mr King, lovely to meet you. I understand you and your wife would like a valuation on this splendid property?'

'That's right.'

'And I hear you've been to stay with Jess. How is she?'

Mandy smiled. 'She's good. She's happy, the baby's eight months now and her business is booming.'

'Wonderful. I keep meaning to pay her a visit. Anyway, if you're ready, where do you want me to start?'

Mandy took care of Chris Jenkins while Trevor took his second glass of wine into the garden and sat on the rattan sofa beneath the rose arch. The evening sun was warm on his face and as he closed his eyes an image of the ideal cottage in the country began to form in his mind: a smaller version of Bracken Farmhouse perhaps, stone-built with views over the expansive countryside. Perfect, as long as they could afford it. He opened his eyes to the brick wall and the house beyond and suddenly felt boxed in. Mandy had cleverly turned their little garden into a sanctuary with colourful flowerbeds filled to bursting but after spending the weekend in the Dales he longed to have some space around him. It would be so good for Mandy and the girls too.

He wondered what his parents would say to them moving. His grandparents had been part of the Windrush generation. It had been tough on them at first, his grandpop working on the buses and his granny taking demeaning cleaning jobs, but Trevor was full of admiration for the way they, and his parents, had grown into the community and raised their families. He thought about the tower block in Pimlico where he grew up and making do with going to the park to kick a ball about. He wanted better for his children. But all in all he didn't have any regrets – it made him appreciate how far he'd come.

Trevor was brought back to the present by Mandy showing Chris Jenkins into the garden. She offered him a drink but he declined. He did a 360 and scribbled away on his clipboard. 'This is magnificent! How long did you say you've lived here?'

Mandy glowed with pride. 'Ten years next month.'

'Well, after looking around, I can safely say that you won't have any trouble attracting buyers. I gather you've made a lot of improvements?'

Mandy and Trevor agreed.

'Splendid. I have clients queuing up for houses like yours in this sought-after area. Where do you plan on moving to?'

Mandy and Trevor exchanged glances. 'The Yorkshire Dales, depending on what we can get for this, of course,' said Trevor.

Chris nodded. 'Ah, Jess has worked her magic. Like I said, you shouldn't have any trouble. I'll have to do a few calculations of course, room sizes and such, but as a ballpark figure, how does eight-hundred-thousand sound?'

Trevor nearly choked on his wine. 'Sounds great.'

Mandy was wide-eyed. The house had more than tripled in value since they'd bought it.

Chris checked his diary. 'OK if I come back tomorrow evening and take some pictures?'

Mandy found her voice, 'Oh, yes. Yes of course.'

'Splendid.'

When Chris Jenkins had gone, Trevor swept Mandy off her feet and gave her a high five. 'Yorkshire Dales here we come!'

# SIX

Jess took out the last of the baking from the Aga and gave herself a mental pat on the back. She'd run out of time yesterday, it was getting too much to do all the baking in one day, but she couldn't bring herself to farm the work out to anyone else. As long as she could keep up with the demand for her three varieties of scone, her many cakes and bakes, she would continue to do it all herself. But she drew the line where baking bread was concerned; she was more than happy to let Sam's son provide her with his delicious crusty bread and rolls.

She poured herself a coffee and sank down on the kitchen sofa. There was something hard in her pocket. She took it out. Oh, yes, the wedding ring Kate had found in the Dog House. She examined the plain yellow gold band. 22 carat! She was tempted to slip it on, see what it felt like. Eddie had never proposed to her but it wasn't that important. Not really. They were happy and that's all that mattered. She looked at the gold band again and wondered: why would anyone leave their wedding ring behind?

She heard Eddie coming across the gravel and shoved the ring back in her pocket.

'Want help with boxing 'em up?' he said, indicating the baked goods.

'In a minute. You hungry?'

'I'm OK for now. We'll sort this lot out first. Eliot still asleep?'

Jess nodded. 'Not for much longer, though.'

'Right, I'll go and get washed and changed.'

There was a knock at the door and in came Kate brandishing a piece of paper. 'Hi Jess, I was talking to the lady who runs the toddler group. I thought you could give her a ring. It's every Tuesday morning in the village hall.' She slapped the piece of paper on the dresser.

Jess glanced at it. 'OK, I'll give her a buzz later.'

'She's there now if you want to phone her, only I told her all about you and she's looking forward to meeting you.'

Jess bristled. There it was again, that pushy attitude. Yes, Jess wanted to get to know other mums but she wanted to do it her way in her own time, not have Kate telling her what to do and how to do it. But on the other hand...

Kate was halfway down the path when Jess called her back. 'Have you got a minute, Kate?'

'Sure.'

'How would you like to run Jessica's Parlour for me once a week?'

'Gosh! On my own, you mean?'

Jess nodded. 'Well, once you'd gotten used to it. Eddie would be on hand of course.'

'Oh! I'd love that!'

'Ok, how about you have a try-out with me and Eddie one morning?'

Kate nodded enthusiastically.

'Awesome. Doing anything tomorrow?'

Kate shook her head. 'What time?'

'Nine-thirty?'

'Thanks Jess, see you tomorrow then.'

Eddie came in from the utility room just in time to see the door closing. 'Who was that?'

'Kate. She gave me the number of the woman who runs the toddler group.'

'And?'

'Well, I asked her to come in tomorrow to help with the coffee, see how she gets on. I might leave her to it once a week.'

Eddie frowned. 'You sure? You always said…'

'Don't have a meltdown. I know what I've always said but I've been thinking about this. I need more time with Eliot and I want to make friends, Eddie. I know you've got other things lined up and, well, with a bit of luck she might be able to do it on her own once she gets the hang of it.'

'I thought we'd discuss it before you made any decisions?'

'We are discussing it.'

Eliot was making his presence felt. Jess shot upstairs to see to her son and Eddie took out the tongs and began boxing up the baked goods.

The phone rang. He stopped mid scone. 'Bracken Farmhouse?'

'Oh, hello,' the woman's voice sounded hesitant, 'I was hoping to speak to Ms Harvey.'

'She's busy right now. Can I help?' He was met with silence. 'Hello?'

The line went dead. Eddie shrugged and put the phone back on its cradle.

Laura Dean quickly shoved her phone back in her handbag and chewed her lip. She didn't want Roger to know what she was doing. She'd try again later. It was a wonder Roger hadn't noticed her wedding ring was missing but, then again, he didn't notice much about her at all these days. It wasn't the first time she'd taken it off – she'd often fantasised about leaving Roger – but this time she'd forgotten to replace it. Now she was feeling anxious in case he questioned her, and she hoped it was still there where she'd left it.

*

Another sunny day and Jessica's Parlour was heaving. Kate was settling in nicely. Jess marvelled at the way she instinctively knew what to do and, as the morning wore on, Jess was feeling quite confident about leaving her in charge one morning a week. Eddie would be there, of course, but it was a relief to know he wouldn't need to be on Kate's tail all the time. She looked as if she was enjoying it too.

Mr Dean screeched to a halt in the car park. Laura had told Roger she wanted to stop off at Jessica's Parlour for coffee on their way home as it was such a lovely day. It would be a bonus if it helped to calm his agitation but, judging by the way he had moaned again about the approach road, she doubted it.

Laura followed her husband through the open front gate, past customers enjoying their morning coffee in the tea garden and into the hallway.

He poked his head round the door of Jessica's Parlour. 'Huh, no tables,' and turned to go.

But Laura was having none of it. 'Why don't we sit outside? I'm sure I saw a vacant table out there.' She went to sit at the only available table.

'Humph, it would be in shade,' said Roger. 'No wonder no one's sitting here.'

Laura tried to ignore his remark. Instead, she concentrated on the ice-cream colour chairs and tables, the pretty garden with the ferns and mind-your-own-business, the classical urns and window boxes full of flowers. The customers sitting to her right were enjoying their morning coffee and some delicious-looking scones, but Roger kept looking at his watch. She hoped he wouldn't get up and leave.

Kate came to take their order. 'Hello, what can I get you?'

'About time,' he grumped. He gave the menu cursory glance and threw it down on the table. 'I'll just have tea.'

Kate looked at Laura.

'A cappuccino and a fruit scone and butter, for me, please.'

'Certainly.' Kate wrote it down on her pad. 'Scones are fresh this morning.'

'I should hope so,' said Roger.

Kate lifted her eyebrows at his remark and scurried away.

Laura saw her chance. 'I need to find a loo. Be back in a minute.'

As she went through to the hallway she almost crashed into Jess coming the other way. 'Oh gosh, I'm terribly sorry.'

'No problem.'

'Actually,' started Laura, 'I suppose you didn't find a ring, by any chance? I think I left it in the Dog House on Sunday.'

Jess's eyes widened. 'Ah, yes, I won't be a tic.'

Laura stood awkwardly in the passage, hoping Roger wasn't timing her. Happy chatter and tinkling cups and saucers drifted from Jessica's Parlour and Laura had a lump in her throat wishing she could enjoy her morning and be happy with her husband. But no, she knew he would never change. This holiday had proved that.

'Here we are.' Jess handed her an envelope.

'Thank you so much.' Laura dropped it into her handbag and went back outside to Roger.

'Where the hell have you been? Your coffee's getting cold.'

She noticed Roger's empty cup. 'There was a queue.' She tried to put on a happy face. 'It's such a lovely, busy little place.'

Roger said nothing in return but looked critically at the surroundings and the golden retriever sitting under the table opposite. 'Huh, they shouldn't allow dogs in eating establishments.'

Laura took a mouthful of coffee. She was on the verge of tears. 'Why do you always have to spoil everything, Roger? Whenever I look forward to something you always put a damper on it.' There. She'd said it. She felt quite liberated. She took her time buttering her scone and savouring every mouthful. Every time they went to a different place Roger's attitude put her off ever going back. But he wasn't going to put her off this one. Not today.

Kate came back. 'Everything all right for you?' she said, looking at the sullen man.

He nodded. 'Finally.'

'Oh dear, I'm sorry you had a wait but we are very busy today.'

'I suggest you get more staff, then.' He threw the money on the table, got up and walked towards the carpark.

'I must apologise for my husband,' said Laura.

Kate shook her head. 'It's clearly not your problem.'

Laura was wondering how long she could stall before following Roger. She wanted to take her time and enjoy the atmosphere of this pretty tea garden in the sunshine. No, she wasn't going to give him the satisfaction of hurrying after him. Too many times she had pandered to his whims and what difference had it made? None! He was like a spoilt child. Popping the last of her scone into her mouth, she looked up to see Roger change direction. He crossed the road and began to walk along the riverbank. She drained her cup and sat back wondering how far he would go.

Her gaze fell on Roger's car keys on the table. Quick as a flash she knew exactly what to do. She ran to the car, shoved it in *drive* and roared up the road. A big smile spread across her face as she saw Roger staring after her in the rear-view mirror.

# SEVEN

After the bright sunny morning the dark clouds had gathered and down came the rain. Visitors who had been sitting in the tea garden had run for cover, either indoors or to their cars. Slowly the tearoom had emptied out and Jess sat down to a proper lunch with Eddie and Eliot instead of snatching a bite in between serving.

It looked as if the rain was set in for the rest of the day. Jess took Eliot upstairs for his nap and the afternoon jogged along calmly until a low-loader drew up in front of Eddie's workshop. He threw on his rain jacket and rushed out to greet the driver.

Eddie had been in touch with Mr Fairview who had told him he had a 1949 Buick lined up if Eddie was interested. He was unsure at first – what would he do with an American car and wouldn't it be more difficult to get the parts? But after doing a bit of research he found a beautiful example on the internet. He learned that there was a lot of support for restorers of American cars and he had warmed to the idea.

Eddie wiped the rain off his face and pulled his hood further over his head while he watched the two guys unload the old car and transfer it into his workshop. After examining the extent of the corrosion, he realised it was in a worse state than he'd been led to believe. To restore this baby back to its original self would be a real challenge. However, there was evidence of the paintwork being a deep burgundy and Eddie's mind conjured up an image of the car in all its glory complete with a white hood and whitewall tyres. Yeah, cool. He paid the driver. 'Cheers, mate.' and watched as the low loader backed down the approach road.

Jess came out to find him. 'There you are.' She looked at the old car that seemed to fill the workshop. 'Blimey! What's this heap of old junk doing here?'

'It might be a heap o' junk now but you wait. It'll be a gleaming showstopper when I've finished with it.'

She stifled a giggle. 'Yeah, right.'

Eddie shook his head. 'Trust me; I'll be able to sell it for five times what I paid for it.'

'What? You *paid* for this? You're joking, right?' Jess walked all around the rusty carcass that sat centre stage. 'I thought you wanted to get into vintage cars, you know, like old Rollers? What is this thing anyway?'

'A 1949 Buick Roadster Convertible, a classic American car, Jess.'

She ran a finger over the folds of the hood and a piece flaked off in her hand. 'Huh, whatever.'

Eddie laughed. 'I'll show you a picture of a pucka job. That'll change your mind.'

They both turned towards the sound of crunching gravel. There was a man heading for the front door. He stood in the porch brushing the rain off his jacket, his hair dripping. On closer inspection, Jess realised it was grumpy Mr Dean. 'Hi, can I help?'

He passed a tissue over his wet face. 'I sincerely hope so.' He blew out a sigh but couldn't meet her eye. 'I've been left without a car and I need to get home. I've been trying to ring for a taxi to take me to the station without any luck. I suppose there's no one here who could give me a lift?'

She watched Eddie go inside the workshop and close the doors. 'No, sorry, Eddie's tied up at the moment and I can't leave the business unattended.'

He looked up and down the drive, along the road. 'In that case do you know of anyone else? Any other taxi firms?'

'Sure, come in.'

He stood dripping on the doormat while Jess searched through the business cards pinned on the cork board in the hall. She gave him a few and showed him into the deserted tearoom.

Jess tried to look busy whilst listening to his calls. Kate had told her how rude he was this morning and how his wife had snatched her chance to get away from him! Yeah, way to go Mrs Dean!

He looked at his phone and sighed heavily. A smile played around Jess's mouth. 'No luck?'

'Yes, in an hour.' He passed a tissue over his hair again. His stomach rumbled. 'I don't suppose I could get something to eat? Only I've had nothing since breakfast.'

'I could make you a sandwich.'

'Fine,' he said with a sigh.

'Tuna and sweetcorn or ham and tomato?'

'Ham and tomato, I can't stand tuna. And I'll have wholemeal bread.'

'Anything to drink?'

'Tea.'

'Oh my God! Did you leave your manners in the car? A please and thank-you wouldn't go amiss.'

'Sorry. It's been one of those days.'

'You're not kidding!'

Jess was tempted to spread the ham with strong mustard but that was pushing it a little too far.

\*

Chris Jenkins stood outside Mandy and Trevor's Victorian semi on Peckham Rye armed with his camera and his paperwork. He was looking forward to giving them the good news and ultimately realising an excellent sale. He was also glad to get out of the office – it had been another uncomfortably warm day. He loosened his tie and rang the bell.

Mandy came to the door. 'Hello, come through. Or would you rather start outside before we lose the sun?'

'Ah, that's an excellent idea.'

'Come round the back when you're ready. The side door's open.'

Chris waited for a break in the traffic and nipped across the road to take some pictures of the front elevation, while Mandy whizzed round to make sure every bottle and jar in the kitchen had been hidden from sight and everything in the living room was just so. She was proud of the improvements they'd made: a sparkling new kitchen extension, a new bathroom and ensuite. They must go some way towards bumping up the price but she had a nagging doubt that Chris Jenkins' ballpark figure was too good to be true. She was hoping Trevor would be able get home in time to hear what Chris Jenkins had to say, but two days in a row was pushing their luck.

Buster jumped up onto the worktop. She grabbed him and plonked him in the living room with Kirsty and Keira and shut the door. Buster and his brother Silvester had been tiny black and white kittens when she first brought them home two years ago. They had both grown into handsome cats and she loved them just as much as the twins did but she drew the line at letting them anywhere near the food prep areas. She smiled remembering the evening when Jess had been blown away by the tiny kittens. She had come to Mandy's to get changed before Giles Morgan's chauffer picked her to take her to his yacht club. That evening had ended in disaster when Giles's estranged wife had burst into the club and embarrassed Jess. Now, there she was, living in the Yorkshire Dales with Eddie and their beautiful little boy, making a go of their business. Mandy was pleased that Jess had come to her senses and let Eddie back into her life instead of continuing the farcical relationship with Giles Morgan.

Mandy finished wiping down the worktops just as Chris opened the patio doors. 'I think I've got some good shots of the front,' he said, checking the screen on his digital SLR. 'Some of the back's in shade but I don't think it'll matter.'

Mandy quickly dried her hands. 'That's good. Do you want to start in here? Then I can get on with dinner.'

'Of course.'

Mandy kept a low profile while Chris clicked away then he opened the door to the living room.

'Take the cats outside,' she told the twins. 'You can come back in a minute.'

'Aw,' moaned Kirsty, 'do we have to?'

'Yes, go on, off you go, just while Mr Jenkins takes some photos.' Mandy quickly plumped up the cushions, turned off the telly and turned on one of the table lamps. Chris took several more pictures and went upstairs.

Mandy turned to see Trevor stride in and throw his keys on the worktop. 'Oh fantastic! I was hoping you'd make it.'

'Has Jenkins said anything, about the price?'

'Not yet.'

Trevor clocked the twins who had come back in from the garden. 'Hi, what you up to? I thought you'd be watching the Disney channel?'

'We were,' said Keira, her mouth downturned, 'but mum told us to come out while that man took photos. Is our house *that* special?'

Trevor smiled knowingly at Mandy.

'Can we go back in now?' asked Kirsty.

'Yeah, off you go.'

Chris came to find Mandy and Trevor. 'Ah, good evening, Mr King. Your house is looking absolutely splendid, a real credit to you and your wife. I'm sure we'll have plenty of interest. After giving it some thought, I recommend we put it on the market for …' he shuffled his paperwork, '…ah, yes, here we are, eight-hundred and ninety-five thousand, five hundred. OK with that?'

'Cool!' said Trevor. Mandy clutched his arm.

'Very good, it should be on the website tomorrow. I'll drop off a copy of the brochure in the next couple of days. If you have any questions don't hesitate to call. Enjoy your evening.' He let himself out through the patio doors.

Trevor braced himself. He had something to tell Mandy but wasn't sure how she'd take it.

# EIGHT

Jess had just put Eliot down for his afternoon nap when Janie burst in through the back door looking fresh-faced and beaming. 'Hi Jess. I hope you don't mind but I've got some fantastic news!'

Jess looked up from chopping some cucumber. 'Fire away.'

'Neptune's on the mend, I can't believe it! The vet's just gone.'

'Oh my God, Janie, that's amazing!' She put the knife down and hugged her.

'Aye, I know. I'm so relieved. Cost me an arm and two legs, mind.'

Jess headed for the tearoom and said over her shoulder, 'Be back in a tic then you can tell me all about it.'

Late lunch for somebody, thought Janie, and tried to ignore her rumbling stomach made worse by the tempting smells wafting around and the fact that her pantry resembled Old Mother Hubbard's. She was disappointed to see Eliot's empty highchair too – seeing that bright little chap made her day.

'Right, Janie', said Jess, clearing a space on the table, 'let's have a cuppa while I've got a minute.'

Janie went to the drinks machine. 'Coffee or tea?'

'Whatever you fancy.'

Janie was hoping Jess would offer her something to eat but she wasn't going to ask. She poured two cups of cappuccino and sprinkled them with powdered chocolate, hoping the rich milky coffee would go some way towards quenching her hunger. She put the coffees down and pulled up a chair. 'Crikey, Jess you're always so busy.'

Jess took a sip of coffee and nodded. 'Yep, and Eddie's playing God to that rust bucket he thinks is going to make him a fortune.'

'What's that?'

Jess shook her head. 'Tell you later. I want to hear all about Neptune.'

'Well, he started to perk up yesterday but I didn't want to get me hopes up, then t' vet called in this morning. He was really surprised. I've still got to keep an eye on him mind, but I think he's over the worst.'

'So what did the vet to do?'

Janie shrugged. 'Nothing much, but his bill won't be!'

'And you can't think why he's got better?'

Janie fiddled with the teaspoon. She wasn't sure how this would go down. 'Well, I did help things along a bit, like.'

'Doing what?'

'A bit of herbal therapy, for horses mainly, but it works for donkeys too.'

Jess looked at her, waiting for more.

'You're going to think I'm crazy.'

'No I won't.'

'OK. I got some plants and laid them in a circle in the paddock then I led Neptune into the centre of them and left him to eat what he wanted.'

Jess raised her eyebrows. 'Is that all?' Janie nodded. Jess sipped her coffee and shrugged. 'Whatever…if it works, go for it.' It did sound a bit wacky but, then again, she knew nothing about donkeys. She suddenly wanted to know more. 'So… what sort of plants?'

'Oh, nothing fancy. It's only things you find in the wild like hawthorn, meadowsweet and clover, but there weren't any in the paddock. I had to go looking for 'em down t' lane. I firmly believe there's a cure for all ills in the wild, Jess…. and horse balls.'

Jess started giggling. 'Horse's what?'

'Horse balls. They're like the fat balls what you give birds, only these are medicinal ones you give horses.'

Eddie breezed in, slipped off his jacket and hung it up. 'Hi Janie, all right?'

She beamed. 'Neptune's better! I were just telling Jess.'

'That's well cool. I'm happy for you.'

'Thanks Eddie.' Janie frowned and looked into her empty cup. 'I don't know how I'm going to pay the vet, mind, not now old PJ's put me rent up again.'

Eddie looked towards the tearoom. 'I think someone wants to pay?'

Jess pushed her chair back. 'I'll go.'

While Eddie had Janie to himself he dug into his pocket and handed her a roll of notes. Janie's eyes were huge. She shook her head. 'Oh Eddie, I can't take that.'

Eddie whispered, 'Yes you can.'

Janie shook her head vigorously.

'OK, how would you like a job, then?'

'What? A paid job... in here... in the tearoom?'

He nodded.

'Oh! Thanks, Eddie. I'll do me best, I really will. I won't let you down. Or Jess.'

Jess looked up from the tray she was carrying in. 'What's going on?'

'I've just given Janie a job,' said Eddie.

'Oh, right. Same drill as before then, Janie – hair, hands, apron.'

'What, now?'

'Yep, no time like the present.'

# NINE

Mandy was at Top to Toe scrolling through *Rightmove* on her phone whilst waiting for a client. After doing some calculations, Trevor had suggested they buy a house in the Dales lower in value than theirs. This would allow them to pay off their mortgage and, being cash buyers, they would be able to snap up the ideal property before anyone else. If they sold before they found a house, they could rent one, which would allow them to take their time and not make any snap decisions.

She knew Jess had taken on a doer-upper but Mandy couldn't envisage living in a caravan while the work was carried out, not with the twins. However, searching for properties today had put a smile on her face. She saved a couple on her phone to show Trevor later. But her mood darkened remembering what he had told her last night – a manager's job had come up in the ideal location but he needed to act quickly if he wasn't going to be pipped at the post.

'It'll mean me moving up there as soon as possible,' he had said, 'even before we sell the house. I can't see another way round it.'

'What? And leave me and the girls here? Oh God, Trev. I'd hate that.'

'I know, but it might not be for long. If Jenkins is right we'll soon sell this. But if push comes to shove...' he had pulled her into his arms and kissed her. 'Maybe you could go live with Carol?'

'Well, let's hope it doesn't come to that.'

Keira had noticed her mum's mood. 'What's wrong, mum?'

'Nothing, love. It's just that your dad might have to move away for a while, that's all.'

'What? Like Sky's dad?'

Mandy had smiled at this – Sky's parents were separated and her mum had a boyfriend. She had reassured Keira that it was nothing like that. Trevor had gathered his family to him, the twins big brown eyes beamed onto his face. 'You know we want to move to the Dales, near Auntie Jess and Uncle Eddie, yeah?'

They nodded and started jumping up and down.

'All right, listen. It might mean I have to take a job up there before we sell the house. Mum will stay here, with you, until we can all be together.'

Keira had frowned. 'But where will *you* live?'

'Well, I'm hoping I can stay with Jess and Eddie.'

Mandy had her reservations. She hoped Jess would come to the rescue, but Mandy knew Jess had a business to run. Although she was sure Jess would love to help them, she wouldn't necessarily give Trevor priority. Also, Mandy wasn't looking forward to dropping the bombshell on her mum on Saturday when she came back from her holiday. The twins were anxious there wouldn't be any ballet classes in the Dales and they were also stressing over Buster and Silvester not liking their new home. Mandy had tried to reassure them. 'Look, don't worry about the cats, they'll soon settle in, and I'm sure they've got ballet classes in the Dales.'

\*

Chris Jenkins ended the call to yet another client looking to buy a substantial property a stone's throw from the city. At this rate he'd soon be able to retire – a nice little pad in the south of France, maybe within walking distance of the beach or the golf course, lazy days in the sun… Yes! Just the ticket. His business had taken a turn for the better these past couple of years, the housing market having picked up, but his office felt a bit flat of late. He missed Jess's sunny smile, her sense of humour and the way she got things done. But he was pleased for her; she deserved a bit of luck. He couldn't help smiling when he recalled how he'd met her. She had answered his advert on the internet for a lady friend and, of course, she was way out of his league. He'd ended up giving her a job instead. Then when she was burgled and couldn't possibly continue living in that grotty flat with the door hanging off, he'd found her a newly refurbished apartment to rent. He also remembered how pleased he was for her when she rang to him with the news that she'd come into money. Yes, he was sorry to lose Jess but it was nice to know she was happy and making a go of her business.

Last week he had advertised for more staff and had been inundated with enquiries. So far, he'd interviewed two smart young women and, although he knew they would be very efficient, they had made him feel old and his office positively archaic. He glanced around at the décor – Jess would have said it seriously needed a facelift – but he couldn't muster the energy or the enthusiasm somehow. At least he could tackle the tired-looking window display. He had given Mr and Mrs King's house prime position in the centre – House of the Week – an enlarged photograph of the attractive front elevation plus smaller ones showing the immaculate interior and the well-stocked garden. It was causing quite a stir – clients were queuing up for viewings – and he was looking forward to showing the first potential buyers around it tomorrow afternoon. Mrs King had assured him she would be there at 3pm.

# TEN

Janie searched through her wardrobe for something to wear for her first day's work in Jessica's Parlour but all of her dresses were mainly calf-length or longer in way-out reds and purples. Jess, she noticed, was always immaculately dressed in smart black jeans or trousers and a pure white tee shirt topped off with her pristine apron with the Jessica's Parlour logo. Janie didn't possess any jeans or trousers but she selected the plainest skirt and top she could find, gave them a sniff and wriggled into them. She stared at her reflection. Not bad, but if she wanted to give a better impression she would have to spend her first week's wages on some new clothes and forego filling her pantry.

She skipped down the narrow stairs and nearly fell headlong over Gandalf. The big tabby flew down to the kitchen and stood waiting by his feeding bowl, staring up at her, tail twitching.

'I'll feed you when I come home, Gandy. I'm late.' Janie picked up her bag, locked her door and hurried up the road. Two cars passed her and pulled into Jess's car park adding to the many already there. She hoped she'd be able to cope – it had been a long time since she'd had a proper job.

As Janie crunched along the gravel drive, she could see all the tables in the tea garden full of people chatting happily in the sun, enjoying their morning coffee and bakes. She opened the door and nearly crashed into Kate. 'Oops, sorry.'

Kate glared at her as if she was something nasty on the sole of her shoe.

'Hi, Janie,' said Jess. 'I see you've met Kate!'

Janie gave Kate her brightest smile but Kate turned her back on her and began taking out her cleaning utensils from the cupboard. Undeterred, Janie nipped to the utility room to find an apron. Suitably attired, she caught Jess's attention, held up her spotlessly clean hands and pointed to her ponytail.

Jess laughed. 'Right, grab a pad and pen and take some orders, OK? It's easy to forget the ones outside so I should start out there first.'

Kate watched Janie as she went through to the tea room. 'Yeah, anyway, I'll get on with the changeovers unless you need me in here?'

'We're OK at the moment, thanks,' said Jess.

Kate craned her neck into the tearoom and grimaced. 'You sure?'

Jess threw her a look. 'Quite sure, thanks Kate.'

Kate's expression said, 'if you say so'. Jess couldn't help comparing the two women. Kate – mega-efficient and tidy at all times and seemed to instinctively know what to do. Janie, on the other hand, needed telling what to do at every turn, but Jess was prepared to let it ride for the time being. Janie was struggling moneywise and Jess knew only too well what that was like.

Eddie breezed in. 'Eliot's a bit feverish, Jess, must be his teeth.'

Janie couldn't help overhearing. 'Maybe you should keep an eye on him?'

'He's teething, poor little bugger. Red-hot cheeks.'

Jess was unconcerned. 'He's fine. What've you got, Janie?'

Janie showed her the orders.

'Right,' said Eddie, 'I'll be in the workshop. Give us a shout if it gets too much.'

*

Mandy gathered the twins and locked her front door. She was looking forward to seeing her mum and hearing all about her cruise, but she wasn't looking forward to telling her they had put their house on the market. Walking along the busy main road a single-decker bus thundered past and Mandy drew the girls away from the edge of the pavement. At least she wouldn't have to worry about the heavy traffic when they moved.

They turned into Goose Green Lane and saw Carol waving to them from her front door. The twins ran the last few yards and into her open arms. She gave them each a kiss and Mandy had to bite back her tears at the thought of leaving her mum behind when they moved.

'Hi, Mum.' Mandy gave her a hug. 'So good to see you. Come on, I want to hear all about your holiday.'

'Just a minute,' said Carol. 'I've got a little something for the twins.' She disappeared and came back with two carrier bags, one each for Kirsty and Keira.

'Oh, God, Mum, they get enough stuff.'

'It's fine.' She winked at them. 'Just a little something I spotted on the trip.'

'Thank you Grandma,' said Keira. Kirsty gave Carol a kiss for hers and they took them into the living room.

'So how was it?' asked Mandy, heading for the kettle.

'Oh, all right. We didn't get long enough in any of the ports though and the ship was massive. You can get lost in all those lounge areas, like a rabbit warren. Something different I suppose but I don't think I'd bother again.' She patted her stomach. 'And the food! I must've put on a stone.'

Mandy glanced through to the living room at the twins sitting on the floor, grinning at each other, with their bright pink backpacks. 'You can use them for your ballet shoes, maybe?'

Carol took two mugs from the cupboard and placed a tea bag in each. 'How was Monika's wedding?'

'Fabulous, you'd have loved it, and the manor was out of this world. Monika's dress was fairy tale, and they made a lovely couple. Jess and Eddie finally managed to get there in the evening but they're so busy. They must be raking it in but she looks knackered.' Mandy was wondering how to break it to her mum they were moving. She would have to choose her moment.

They took their mugs of tea into the living room where Kirsty and Keira now sat munching their way through a packet of sweets.

'Where did you get those?' asked Mandy. Carol looked sheepishly at her. 'Well, don't make a meal of 'em, you'll spoil your tea.'

Through the open window the roar of the relentless traffic reminded her that she and Trevor were doing the right thing. She took a sip of tea and braced herself. 'God, it's so noisy here. I notice it more since we've been away.'

Carol shrugged it off. 'I suppose it is, but I've got used to it.'

Mandy glanced at Kirsty and Keira and thought she'd better say something before they did. 'Mum, I don't know what you think to this, but Trevor and I are thinking of moving up there, to the Dales.' She let that sink in before she went any further. Her mum had put down her mug and was threading and unthreading her fingers. 'Trevor's asked for a transfer.'

Carol bit her lip. 'Oh, right. I knew it would happen one day. Peckham's not the best place to bring up a family. Oh, it's improved over the years, but it can't compare to life in the country. I should know, I was brought up in the Garden of England, don't forget.'

Mandy was heartened by this. 'What? You wouldn't mind?'

'No, I didn't say that. I would miss you all dreadfully, you know that. I'd just have to put up with it, wouldn't I?'

'But you could come up for holidays. We're hoping to get a big enough place so you can have your own room, maybe even your own annexe.'

Carol brightened. 'Really? Can you afford it?'

Mandy beamed. 'Chris Jenkins said ours is worth…wait for it…eight-hundred-and-ninety-five-thousand pounds!'

'What?'

'Yep, I know. I still can't believe it.'

Carol looked down at her hands. 'Right, sounds like it's all going ahead, then?'

'Aw, don't get upset, Mum. We'll come down as often as we can and, anyway, it might be ages before we sell it. Some houses stay on the market for up to two years.' Mandy hoped she hadn't jinxed it saying this.

Carol glanced out the window as another bus went thundering down the road. 'You are doing the right thing, love, it'll be much better for the twins. I'll just have to get used to it, that's all.'

Mandy took out her phone to show her mum the type of house they were looking for, hoping that some of her excitement would rub off and soften the blow. 'I've seen some lovely places on *Rightmove*. Here, look at these.'

Chris Jenkins knocked again on Mandy and Trevor's door, huffed and checked his watch. He was sure he had arranged for Mrs King to meet him at 3pm. It was now 3:15. This was most embarrassing. He looked at the couple standing in the front garden. 'I'm really sorry. Mrs King assured me she would be here. I'll try her again.' He rang Mandy's number but it went straight to voicemail.

'Haven't you got a key?' asked the man.

'No, I was under the impression Mr and Mrs King wanted to be in full control.'

'Well, we've got a house in Dulwich to view at 4 o'clock,' said the young woman, and they turned to go.

'I'll rearrange the viewing,' said Chris, desperately hoping he wouldn't lose their custom.

Mandy hurried along the road. She had been so engrossed in showing her mum the houses on her phone that she'd forgotten all about the time. 'I'm so sorry,' she panted, running up to her front door. 'I got held up at work,' she lied. She quickly unlocked the door and showed them in. They were making all the right noises, but she was kicking herself.

# ELEVEN

Jess strapped a none-too-happy Eliot into his buggy and set off down the drive. She'd been in two minds whether to go to Toddlers today but she'd rung Molly, the woman who ran the sessions, and she was looking forward to meeting her. Even so, Jess felt a bit apprehensive. She'd never had much to do with other mums and their children. Since having Eliot she hadn't had a minute to breathe.

It was another sunny morning and she hoped Kate and Janie would hit it off and be able to cope with the demand. She needed to let go once in a while. When she left, Sam had been sitting in his usual spot with his mug of tea, watching the proceedings. Jess thought there was probably more to him than met the eye but, then again, she'd never had the chance to have a proper chat with him.

She took a deep breath and pushed Eliot through the double doors. A forceful but cheery-looking woman in a green flowery shirt and leggings came rushing towards them.

'Hi! I'm Molly. So glad you could make it,' she gushed. She bent down to Eliot's level. 'So, this is Eliot?' He screamed in her ear. 'He's adorable.'

'Yeah,' said Jess, watching her restless son trying to wriggle out of his buggy. 'He's teething so he's a bit... grouchy.' She was going to say pissed but thought better of it.

'Well, come and meet the others,' said Molly. 'Eliot is probably the youngest but don't let that put you off. It's good to start them young.'

The doors swung open and in came a man with a baby in the buggy and a little girl who looked about two. Jess couldn't imagine Eddie at Toddlers.

The others were all getting into a circle, sitting cross-legged on the floor. Jess found a space and sat down with Eliot on her lap. It was mayhem; the mums trying to hear themselves speak while their kids ran amuck.

'Listen up everyone,' shouted Molly, trying to make herself heard over the din, 'we have two new members this morning – Jess and Eliot.'

All eyes turned to Jess with a collective, 'Hi'. The woman sitting next to Jess introduced herself. 'I'm Ramona. How old is your little boy?'

'Eight months.' Jess looked around at the other children. Some were running about, some were crawling. 'I feel like the odd one out.'

'Aw, don't worry. You'll soon slot in. Mine's over there,' she said, pointing to a little girl who was making another one cry. 'Yeah, Poppy's a bit of a bully!' She jumped up and went to sort out the problem.

Jess was hoping for some sort of structure to the session but it looked like one big free-for-all. Most of the women were in leggings and baggy tops, none of them wore any make-up and Jess felt like a supermodel in comparison, having straightened her hair and put on her best pair of skinny jeans and figure-hugging tee shirt.

'I'll let you introduce yourselves,' said Molly, throwing back her head of curly brown hair, 'I'll just go and check on the water boiler. It's a bit temperamental.' This was directed at Jess, and she couldn't help watching Molly fiddle with the dial on the ancient-looking urn.

Eliot was sucking his thumb and was almost asleep. Jess felt his cheeks and his forehead; they were hot and clammy.

'Teething?' asked Ramona.

Jess nodded. 'About time. He's only got one tooth, at the bottom.'

'Poppy got her first two at four months. They're all different, aren't they?'

Molly plonked herself in the centre of the circle. 'OK! What do the wheels on the bus do?'

One little boy shouted, 'They go round and round.'

'Very good, Thomas.'

Everyone started singing. Jess felt compelled to join in, but she couldn't help thinking the mums were enjoying the sing-song far more than the kids who were running about and doing their own thing. They came to the end of the song and broke into, *Row, Row, Row Your Boat* then *Incy Wincy Spider*. There was a short break to let everyone get their breath back then Molly started singing, *If You're Happy and You Know It, Clap Your Hands*. Eliot was definitely not happy. Jess cuddled him and stroked his forehead.

During the next few minutes the songs ramped up to fever pitch and the children got more boisterous until Molly said, 'Right, I think we'll break for a much-needed cuppa.'

She turned to Jess. 'We help ourselves. Cups on the table and I've put some biscuits out. Donations welcome but don't feel you have to.'

There was a stampede to the table leaving Jess sitting on the floor cuddling Eliot among the toddlers whose noise levels knew no bounds. Eliot looked at her reproachfully. She brushed his damp hair off his forehead and kissed his hot cheek. 'I know, sweetheart. We'll go home in a minute.' She wasn't ecstatic about having a cup of lukewarm instant coffee and a stale biscuit either, when she could go home for one of her own Americanos and a freshly baked scone. In fact, that wasn't bad idea.

She strode over to Molly with Eliot screaming. 'I think I'll take him home. He's a bit feverish.'

'Oh dear, that's a shame. You *sure* you can't stay?'

Jess shook her head. 'I'm a bit worried about him to be honest. He's very hot.'

'Right,' Molly turned on her phoney cheesy grin, 'See you next week?'

Jess nodded and put the now howling Eliot in his buggy. She was out of there like a shot leaving the fracas behind.

Pushing open the back door she found Kate and Janie at loggerheads.

Kate glared at Jess. 'I refuse to work with her! She's broken a cup, spilt coffee all over the floor and forgotten all about the customers outside. One couple were so fed up of waiting they left!'

Janie was in tears and Eddie was nowhere to be seen. 'Right, I'll be back in a minute.' She strode across to the workshop with Eliot still screaming in her ear.

Eddie rolled out from under the Buick. 'Wassup?'

Jess blew out a sigh. 'Well, Kate and Janie are ready to kill each other and we've lost some customers.'

'Oh shit.' Eddie wiped his oily hands on a rag. 'I only left 'em for a minute.' He followed Jess back to the kitchen and went to the utility room to scrub his hands while Jess took Eliot upstairs.

Kate was rushing back and forth with a cheery smile, while Janie was in a terrible state.

'Come on, girls. What's this all about?' said Eddie, but Kate ignored him and took a tray of food through to the tea garden. He looked at Janie's tear-stained face. 'Come on Janie. It can't be that bad, can it?'

'Oh, Eddie, I'm really sorry,' she sniffed. She leant forward to check Kate was out of earshot and whispered, 'I really, really want this job, but she's been a bitch ever since I walked in.'

'OK, look, wait till Jess comes down. We'll sort it.'

Janie tried to pull herself together. She couldn't look at Kate. She hadn't liked the look of Eliot either but she didn't know if she should say anything. She knew it was none of her business but she couldn't help feeling anxious for the little boy or for Jess and Eddie. The memory of what happened to her little brother was like a warning beacon.

Kate came back, huffed and looked daggers at Janie, pinned two more orders to the dresser and took another tray though to the tearoom.

Jess rushed in with her hair tied up. 'Poor little boy, I knew I shouldn't've taken him out this morning.'

'You weren't to know, love,' said Eddie. 'Is it his teeth?'

Jess nodded. 'I think so, but he's burning up.'

Janie couldn't hold back any longer. After all, they might thank her in the long run. 'Maybe you should phone the doctor? I don't want to worry you but me little brother looked very similar when he were took bad.'

Jess and Eddie both stared at her. 'What you saying, Janie?' asked Jess.

Janie clapped a hand to her mouth, unsure whether she should say any more. But to be forewarned was to be forearmed. 'I don't know if you want to hear this, but Freddie were about same age when he contracted meningitis. Has Eliot got a rash? Is he sleepy? Refusing his feeds?'

'Oh my God!' said Jess. 'Is it fatal?'

'Not if it's caught in time.' Janie looked down at her soggy tissue. 'Freddie...' and burst into tears again.

Jess rang the health centre while Eddie took Janie into the conservatory and sat her down. 'How is it you've never mentioned this before?'

Janie shook her head, 'I don't know, but I thought it only fair to warn yer. When I get these strong feelings it's like I get 'em for a reason.' She studied Eddie's face. 'I'm sorry, Eddie.'

'No, no you did right. But what happened to Freddie?'

Janie's bottom lip wobbled. 'He died.'

'Oh God, I'm so sorry Janie.'

She dried her eyes and blew her nose. 'It's OK. Long time ago now. But I used to take him everywhere with me. I were fourteen. I used to help me mam – there were six of us and she were run off her feet, bless her.'

Jess came in to find them. 'I'm taking him round there now. Dr Sanders said it was probably his teeth but she'd check him over to be on the safe side. Thanks Janie.'

Janie screwed up her eyes and nodded.

# TWELVE

Mandy hugged her mobile to her after speaking to Chris Jenkins. There had been a lot of interest in their property. Apparently he had two more clients lined up and he'd asked Mandy if one of them could pop round this evening and if she would mind showing them around without him?

She hurried home from work, determined not to blow it this time, and did a quick recce on the house. It all looked OK, they weren't an untidy family, but the twins had left their toys in the middle of the living room. She quickly gathered them up and stuffed them into the ottoman. Next she rang her mum to ask her to bring the twins home after they'd had their tea instead of going to collect them. She wasn't going to be caught out again – she was still smarting from screwing up last time.

Trevor's mobile went straight to voicemail, so Mandy left a message telling him about the viewing. She flew round with the vacuum cleaner then padded into the kitchen to make a cup of tea. Glancing at the shiny white units and black worktops she wrung out a cloth and made doubly sure there were no crumbs left behind and then stood back to admire her elegant kitchen. The sun was on the front of the house but here at the back it was in shadow. Lights on or off, she wondered, then decided to leave them off in case it sent out the wrong message. She noticed some cat hairs on the armchair cushion where Buster had been and quickly hoovered them up. There was no sign of him, probably out hunting, and she hoped he wouldn't grace the living room with a half-eaten mouse any time soon. Silvester was curled up on the sofa and looked so peaceful she couldn't bring herself to kick him out in the garden. She fetched her now cooled tea from the kitchen and sat down to stroke the cat. He began to purr, glanced up at her briefly and tucked his nose under his tail.

Mandy heard a car draw up outside and braced herself. Should she stand at the door ready to let them in or should she not look too eager? Trevor still wasn't home but she knew she should be able to do this on her own. How hard could it be?

The doorbell shrilled and Mandy took a deep breath. Two guys stood in the porch. The tall one spoke. 'Mrs King? Hi, pleased to meet you, Gary and Todd.'

Mandy showed them through to the kitchen. 'Would you like to start in here?'

'That would be great,' said Gary, 'we love to cook.' Todd nodded.

Mandy wasn't sure if she should point out the up-to-the-minute features or just leave them to it. But she was shocked when they started looking in the ovens and opening the cupboards, discussing how they could redesign the kitchen. Bloody cheek! It was all perfectly *workable* as far as she was concerned.

Ignoring Mandy, the guys marched into the living room and again, spoke to each other as if Mandy wasn't there. 'Looks a bit tired. Maybe rip out the fireplace, the coving and the ceiling rose?' said Gary, 'give it some clean lines?'

Todd agreed. 'Yeah and strip the floors. I assume it's floorboards and not concrete?'

Mandy wanted to cry. The beautiful period features were one of the reasons they had chosen the house.

On the landing she stood back while they poked around in the bathroom and again Gary wanted to change everything and replace the bath with a walk-in shower. Mandy had fond memories of bathing the twins in there when they were babies. She could feel her anger rising.

'Well,' she said, 'I could show you the garden but there's not much point.' She went downstairs, wrenched open the front door just as Trevor came up the path. The two guys ignored him and got into their car.

'That went well, then?' said Trevor.

Mandy shook her head in dismay. 'They want to rip it to shreds. I don't care how much they offer, they are not having it!'

*

Eddie padlocked his workshop and strolled into the utility room to wash his hands. The Buick was shaping up nicely. He was looking forward to proving to Jess how wrong she'd been.

He opened a can of beer, slumped on the sofa and took a long swig to wash the dust out of his throat. He could hear Jess upstairs putting Eliot to bed. He would've gone with her to the doctors' this morning but something had told him not to leave Kate on her own. Thankfully Dr Sanders had confirmed Eliot was only teething and there was no indication to suggest otherwise. They had cried with relief but this scare had left them with another dilemma. Although Kate worked well, Jess didn't like her attitude and she hated the way she treated Janie. In the end they had agreed to give Janie Tuesdays off leaving Kate in charge on the Toddler Group mornings and see how it went from there.

Jess came in, ran a hand through her hair and blew out a sigh.

'How is he?' asked Eddie.

'Still a bit feverish but at least he's asleep. I gave him some *Calpol*.'

'You look knackered, love. Go and put your feet up. Here, take this with you.' He poured her a large glass of ice-cold pinot grigio.

She planted a thank-you kiss on his cheek. 'God, what a day.'

'I know, right. Go and chill and I'll call you when dinner's ready.'

Jess and Eddie very rarely used the lounge – everything centred on and around the kitchen, the hub of the house – but Jess loved this high-ceilinged room with its period features. When she first opened Bracken Farmhouse she had used this room as a shop to showcase her odd pieces of furniture and table lamps but, after a few months, she had decided that these would be better put to use in the two holiday barns, leaving this room for relaxation, or 'best room' as her nan would've called it. Huh! What would she have thought to her granddaughter now?

Jess tucked her feet up on the plush pale blue sofa, took a mouthful of the chilled white wine and felt the tension of the day slowly subside. Through the Georgian window the evening sun shone onto the large oil painting above the fireplace. She smiled, remembering the first time she had seen it. Giles had invited her to his Greenwich apartment and she had been drawn to the painting of Coverdale in its heavy gilt frame. It turned out that the artist was Edward Clarke and Jess's ancestor, Emma, was the sleeping figure beneath the tree. After some digging into their family history, she and her sister Shelley had discovered that Emma and Edward had had an affair and, Walter, their great- grandfather, had been their illegitimate offspring. It was he who had left Jess and Shelley the unexpected legacy. This painting of Coverdale had gone missing many years ago, but Lydia, Giles's ex-wife, had insisted it belonged to her. It transpired that Lydia was Jess and Shelley's distant cousin, although, not wanting to be associated with the poorer branch of the family, Lydia had denied it. That suited Jess – she had no desire to run into Lydia again! Jess had never forgotten the evening when The Bitch from Hell had stormed into Giles's yacht club and embarrassed her. When Giles knew that Jess was planning to move to the Dales, Giles had given her the painting. Jess loved the fact that she now lived very close to the place where it had been painted.

Jess took another mouthful of wine and cosied-up in the cushions. She was so relieved that Eliot was only teething. She didn't know what she'd have done if the doctor had confirmed her fears. Poor Janie, it must've been heart-wrenching to stand by and watch her little brother get sick and die. And her poor mother run ragged with all those kids to look after. Jess felt sympathy for Janie; coming from a similar background, she knew only too well what it was like to scrimp and scrape to make ends meet. Jess didn't know much more about her other than that she lived in a rented two-up-two-down cottage with only her tabby cat for company, but Jess decided she should get to know her better and maybe pay her a visit one evening.

*

Janie called Neptune and Pluto over to give them some treats. She loved the way they came at her beckoned call, more like two faithful dogs than two donkeys. She held out her flat palm with the pellets, first to Neptune and then Pluto. She was so pleased that her herbal therapy had worked on Neptune. She'd always had a soft spot for donkeys, right from when her mam took her and her siblings to Scarborough on one of the few occasions when she'd had a few coppers to spare. Janie remembered the donkeys as if it were yesterday: their friendly faces, their coarse coats and the comforting rhythm as they plodded along the sand. But these two were never going to work again and Janie loved caring for them and seeing them happy. She topped up their water trough and blanked out the thought of what would happen if she could no longer afford to keep them.

Janie shielded her eyes against the beam of orange sunlight slowly sinking below the distant hills. A blackbird, perched high up on her chimney pot, was competing with another for the loudest song. This was the best part of the day for Janie, the promise of new beginnings. While the bright pink and purple clouds of the sunset slowly faded, she made a wish and trudged back to the cottage.

Kicking off her muddy boots, Gandalf came running up to her. 'Hello, Gandy. I expect you're hungry too?' The tabby purred loudly and rubbed himself against her legs. She stroked his thick fur and tore open a pouch of cat food. There were only two more left. She needed that job at Jess's. She would like to work there every day, but she was damned if she was going to work with Kate! Janie had picked up the vibes that she wasn't exactly flavour of the month where Jess was concerned either. Janie wondered if she might try and help things along a bit. She made a cuppa with a used tea bag, lit some incense sticks and sat cross-legged on the rag rug in front of the fireplace. Taking a moment to get into the zone she opened her book of spells.

# THIRTEEN

Feeling more confident than usual, Janie said hello to Sam sitting in his usual spot cradling his mug of tea, and went to the utility room to don her apron and scrub her hands. Sam watched her every move. He'd heard on the grapevine what had happened the other day. 'Are you all right, lass?'

She nodded.

'It's none of me business, but I think you need to watch Kate.'

'Thanks Sam but I think I've got it sorted.'

Jess was surprised to see her all kitted out and ready to go. 'Oh, hi Janie. All right?'

'Yes ta. I hope yer don't mind but I've started table four.'

'No, carry on,' said Jess.

Janie looked around. 'Where's Eddie?'

'Give you three guesses.'

Janie raised her eyebrows and took the prepared tray to the table by the window, set down the food and drinks with a cheery smile and went to see if the people outside had ordered. She wasn't going to fall foul of that one again! There were four elderly ladies sitting outside in the sunshine. Their conversation ceased and all eyes turned to Janie as she stepped over the threshold. 'Good morning. Have you ordered?'

'Yes, thank you,' said a portly woman with grey hair. 'Such a lovely place you have here.'

Janie smiled sweetly. 'Thanks, I'll pass it on.' She began clearing another table whilst keeping an ear to their conversation.

'We ought to make this our regular coffee morning,' said another. 'Have you seen inside?'

'Yes, very pretty, but it's too nice to sit indoors today.'

'Perhaps we could bring our book group here for lunch one day?'

'That's a brilliant idea…'

Back in the kitchen, Sam had disappeared and Jess was putting the finishing touches to a tray of coffees. 'Here you are, Janie, for the ladies outside. I just need to nip over the workshop. Be back a in a tic.'

Janie noticed that Eliot wasn't there. 'How's Eliot?'

'A bit better, thanks. He's catching up on some sleep. Ha! Wish I could! I'll be glad when those teeth come through.'

'I bet he will too!'

Janie took the tray out to the four ladies, taking care not to slop any coffee in the saucers, and placed them carefully on the table.

'I forgot to ask you for some fresh milk,' said the portly woman. 'I hate UHT.'

'We only serve fresh semi-skimmed,' said Janie, putting a jug on the table, 'unless you want dairy-free, soya or almond. Can I get you anything else?'

'Our scones?'

'Oops, sorry!' Janie felt the blood rush to her cheeks. 'Back in a jiffy.'

When Janie returned with their food, the four women looked as if they were enjoying their morning and so was she. Without Kate scrutinising her every move and her snide remarks Janie was feeling much happier and the tearoom had an element of calm. Just as it should be.

\*

Laura Dean's mother had invited her to lunch at Claridge's. After her disastrous holiday with Roger, chatting over some delicious food and wine had been exactly what she needed. At first, Laura hadn't wanted to offload her troubles, she didn't want her mother to know the extent of her problems, but after three glasses of merlot she began to relax and thought why-the-hell not? She was fed up with pussy-footing around, pretending everything was perfect in her marriage. It was about time Marjorie knew the truth. As it turned out, Marjorie was completely on her side and had thrown her head back in glee when Laura recounted how she'd literally left Roger standing.

As she sipped her coffee, Marjorie listened intently as Laura continued her story.

'When I turned the key in the front door I had a huge sense of satisfaction, although I did feel a bit guilty. I wasn't looking forward to his reprimand either.'

'Well, it sounds to me like he got everything he deserved.'

Encouraged by this remark, Laura took a sip of coffee and continued. 'Two hours later he came in and went straight upstairs without saying a word. Although he's never been violent, I was worried about what he would do when he came down, but he made himself some beans on toast, took it up to his study and ignored me for the rest of the evening. He's been sleeping in the guest room ever since. I don't know what's worse – his stiff comments or his complete detachment.' Laura blew out a sigh and fiddled with her teaspoon. 'I'm so fed up with his self-righteous attitude. I'm at the end of my tether. What am I going to do?'

'Well, dear, if you want my advice, I think you should indulge yourself in a little project to take your mind off it. Divorce is a messy business; the only people who gain are the lawyers. I'd stay well clear.' Before Laura could protest, Marjorie went on, 'What you need is a life within a life, not go looking for ways to get out of it.' She studied her daughter's demeanour; she looked very downcast. 'How about opening a little boutique somewhere? It would give you an interest, also your own income.'

Laura brightened. Maybe her mother had a point. Laura couldn't imagine Roger agreeing to a fair divorce settlement; he was far too selfish for that. She didn't think she could bear his recriminations either. She hadn't worked for years, hadn't needed to, but the idea of her own place and her own money began to worm its way under her skin. She began to picture a little shop, maybe with accommodation, selling pretty things, being her own boss.

'I'll lend you the money to set it up. You needn't pay me pack until you're making a profit.'

A big smile settled on Laura's face. 'Are you sure?'

Marjorie nodded. 'Of course. And when you're up and running I'll be your first customer!'

Heartened by this, Laura went home and immediately opened her laptop. Before she got married she had worked for an estate agent so she had a pretty good idea of what sort of premises to look for but, after searching for hours, she was becoming disheartened. It would be so easy to give up but she kept reminding herself that Roger would never change. Her mother's advice was ringing in her ears and the more she thought about it the more Laura was determined to have her own life but perhaps London wasn't the place to do it. All the available premises she'd seen so far were either too big or too expensive or in the wrong place. Besides, she really wanted to get as far away as possible from Roger.

She made a cup of tea, took it into the lounge and sat looking out of the window at the garden. She thought about all the places she had loved but that Roger had turned her against. The list was endless but the one that kept popping up was the most recent one in the Dales, such a pretty place and in such a lovely village. She felt her heart lift. Yes! She would book a room at Bracken Farmhouse and go in search of her ideal property.

\*

Feeling in need of a little lift, Carol was treating herself to a shopping spree in Oxford Street. She had been looking forward to meeting up with her friends for a good old chinwag but neither June nor Sue was able to join her today and the experience so far had fallen a bit flat. The noisy, dirty streets were brought to her notice, and everything was either over-priced or not to her taste. She couldn't help thinking how different all it was from the 1970s; shopping in Chelsea Girl in Carnaby Street and C&A at Marble Arch, the fashions so crisp and bright. Those were the days! All the clothes she'd seen today looked as if someone had slept in them and the shoes were another story.

Carol decided to console herself with a cup of coffee and a cake in *Café Nero*. Gone were the Wimpy Bars of her youth where she would meet up with friends in her lunch hour and the jazz club with the hope of finding a nice-looking chap to ask her out. She crushed the memory of her one true love, baulked at the price of an Americano and a chocolate muffin, bought them anyway and took a seat at the only vacant table.

A few minutes later Carol looked up to see a young woman standing opposite. 'Is anyone sitting here?'

Carol shook her head. 'No, go ahead.'

Judging by her designer handbag, her immaculate nails and glossy hair, thought Carol, the woman wasn't short of a few bob. Carol self-consciously hid her old woman hands under the table and watched the woman-about-town scroll earnestly through her phone. Carol was on the point of leaving her to it when she overheard her make contact with a person on the other end.

'Oh, hello, Bracken Farmhouse?'

Now, where had she heard that name before?

# FOURTEEN

Mandy and Trevor were getting ready for another viewing. He had managed to wangle the afternoon off and Mandy's last two clients had cancelled. The twins were at Carol's and both cats were out. Boo-yah! Mandy had flown round with the vacuum cleaner whilst Trevor made sure everything was in its proper place. The weather wasn't ideal, having rained all night, but they hoped it wouldn't deter their prospective buyers. Standing side by side in the kitchen, they gave each other a high five and waited for the doorbell to ring.

'Third time lucky, yeah?' said Trevor.

'Let's hope so,' said Mandy. Even though it hadn't been long since they'd put the house on the market, she was finding the house-selling palaver a lot more stressful than she'd imagined. Mandy still didn't like the idea of Trevor moving up to the Dales without her but if these people today fell in love with the house they could start to make plans. Even Carol kept asking how the viewings were going.

At two minutes to three the doorbell shrilled.

'You going?' asked Trevor.

Mandy pasted a welcoming smile on her face and opened the door to a young couple who stepped inside and shook hands with her, the woman proudly showing off an advanced bump.

'Evie and Reece,' said the young man. 'Lovely to meet you.'

Mandy led them through to the kitchen. Reece went directly to the patio doors to peer out at the garden, while Evie stood centre stage and did a 360. Her smile said it all. She caught her husband's attention. 'Wow, this is lovely! What do you think, darling?'

He turned back to his wife. 'Yeah, I like it. And just look at that garden!'

Mandy gave Trevor a quick I-can't-believe-it look and showed them into the living room.

'Oh, this is glorious,' said Reece, 'so light and airy and I'm glad you've kept the period features.'

Mandy was relieved, 'Thank you. It was one of the reasons we bought the house.'

'And you've been happy here?'

'Oh yes, it's just that we want to move up north.'

Reece nodded. 'I noticed the patio doors out to the garden. Can we?'

'Of course.' Mandy tried not to count her chickens as she slid open back the door to reveal her beloved garden in all its glory, the sun now highlighting the raindrops like a million jewels.

'Oh wow! This is amazing!' said Evie, exploring every corner. 'I could lose myself out here. And I love that rose arbour, look darling.'

Reece went to join her. 'Mmm, a nice glass of wine on a warm sunny evening? Just the job,' he said, gazing around.

The words 'family home' reached Mandy's ears and she felt a shiver down her spine.

Trevor showed the couple upstairs while Mandy put the kettle on. She had a feeling this couple wouldn't be leaving any time soon.

*

Jess went up for a quick shower while Eddie cleared away the remains of their evening meal. She had been thinking about dropping in on Janie all afternoon. She hadn't rung in case something cropped up, but she didn't think Janie would mind if she popped in on the off-chance. And even if she was out Jess would enjoy a refreshing stroll through the village, something she rarely got time for these days. Jess and Eddie had had a few sleepless nights with Eliot and, what the business to run, it had all started to get on top of her. With a bit of luck, chilling at Janie's might be just what she needed.

She quickly got dressed and flashed the hairdryer over her long blonde hair, applied a lick of make-up and ran downstairs, grabbed her phone and kissed Eddie goodbye.

The evening was still warm as she set out along the drive. Further along, she noticed the state of the approach road. Was it her imagination or were the potholes getting worse? She hadn't noticed them when she took Eliot to toddlers, but she would definitely have to look into it. She didn't want her guests to get the wrong impression.

As she approached the Green Man a blackbird was singing high up in the oak tree, people sitting in the garden with children and dogs, all enjoying their summer evening. She glanced through the gate and tried to catch Greg's attention, but he was too busy to notice her.

The sound of giggling made her turn towards the river where some children on the footbridge were playing Pooh Sticks and she wondered how long it would be before she was able to do that with Eliot. Two hikers passed her with a 'Good evening,' and went on their way. Three more people sped past her on bikes. She stood for a moment to drink in the scene, to feel the evening sun on her skin and to breathe in the fresh scents of the countryside.

At the end of the row of terraced cottages she found Janie's. It didn't look as though anyone used the front door so she went round the side and knocked. While she waited, Jess noticed the general state of neglect – the cracked concrete path, the peeling paint. Old PJ needed to stick his hand in his pocket and get some repairs done, the old skinflint. A big tabby cat came running up to her, meowing, and as soon as the door opened the cat shot past her.

'Hi Jess,' said Janie, standing aside. 'What took you so long?'

Jess frowned.

'Oh, it's just… I had a feeling you'd be round tonight.'

'Really?'

'Aye. Anyway, come in.'

Jess was still coming to terms with this revelation as she followed Janie into her living room. She also felt seriously underdressed. Janie had gone all out tonight with a long floaty pink and purple number, rows of beads swinging from her neck and colourful bangles jangling at her wrist. She seemed a totally different person in her own environment.

'Tea?'

Jess nodded. 'Please.'

'Have a seat.' Janie parted a beaded curtain to access the space that Jess assumed was the kitchen. She perched on the edge of the only armchair covered with a purple and gold throw and felt totally out of place. She glanced around. Although the brick fireplace was small it seemed to dominate the room. The only other furniture consisted of a wicker stool and an old wooden dining chair. A small TV perched on a low table but the lighted candles dotted about made the front room oddly comforting. The big tabby came and sat at Jess's feet, licked his paws and began to wash his face. She could never resist stroking a cat and this one was gorgeous.

Janie came back with two mugs of tea and placed one beside Jess. 'Oh, I see you've met Gandalf.'

'He's lovely.'

'Mm, he's a big softie. He likes you. Cats are very intuitive, you know.' Janie sat on the dining chair and took a sip of tea.

'Have you had him from a kitten?'

'No, he just walked into me life one day and stayed. How's Eliot?'

'Much better, thanks. He went off to sleep as good as gold tonight. Nearly got all his front teeth through now.'

'That's good.'

Jess was at a loss to know what else to talk about. She didn't want to discuss the tearoom and definitely not Kate. 'So, how long have you lived here?'

Janie shrugged. 'I dunno, must be going on ten year, maybe more.' She noticed the way Jess's eyes travelled around the room. 'It's not much but it suits me and I've got the paddock for Neptune and Pluto.'

Jess nodded, taking it all in. 'Is Neptune OK now?'

'Aye, still got t' vet on me tail, though.'

Jess sipped the hot weak tea. 'Not being funny Janie, but how do you manage?'

'Same as I always have. I don't need much; as long as me animals are happy that's all I care about. The vet will just have to take a back seat that's all.'

Jess's curiosity was getting the better of her. There was no evidence of a man in Janie's life, or woman for that matter. From where she sat she couldn't see anything that suggested another person shared the house. 'What about your love life? Only you've never let on.'

Janie stood up. Jess thought she'd overstepped the mark until Janie said, 'Let's sit outside, it's too nice to be in here.' She led the way through to the little garden where a metal table and two slatted chairs balanced on some uneven paving. As she sat down, Jess noticed a patch of herbs, a tiny, raised bed full of vegetable plants and a rickety shed. A picket fence divided this garden from the paddock where the donkeys stood munching their hay.

'I'm out here a lot in the summer,' said Janie. 'I like being surrounded by nature, at one with the elements.' She drained her mug and set it on the table.

Jess was hanging onto hers like a lifeline. She hadn't expected to feel so awkward although she knew all along that there was something different about Janie.

'Anyway', said Janie, 'getting back to me love life…'

'Oh God, look, I'm sorry, you don't have to…'

Janie shook her head. 'It's fine, really. I don't often get the chance to talk about Denny. There, I've actually said his name.'

Jess didn't want to keep prying but she was all ears. She set her mug of half-drunk tea on the rusty table and waited for Janie to enlighten her.

'I met Denny when the fair came to town. I had a friend I used to hang out with sometimes when me mam didn't need me to do the chores. It were her idea. I'd never been to a fairground before and I were bowled over by the bright lights, the music, people enjoying themselves. I could've stayed all night. Then Masie dragged me into the fortune teller's hut, said it would be a laugh. I weren't sure at first. We sat in the waiting area, all calm and soft tinkling music, until Madam Rose called me in. Me eyes were everywhere! I'd never seen anything like it. She was wearing a brightly beaded headscarf and sitting behind a table covered with a shimmering purple cloth. She gave me a crystal ball to hold while she spoke to me. She seemed to know so much about me it were unreal.'

Jess realised she was gaping. 'So, what did she tell you?'

'Well, she said I were going to meet a dark handsome stranger.' She grinned at Jess. 'Yeah, I know, the usual stuff! But I were that gullible back then. I came out in a daze. Then, on the waltzer, I climbed up and sat down with Masie and this gorgeous-looking fella appeared from nowhere, flashed his smile and took me last 50p.' She smiled and gazed into the distance.

'What happened?'

'He asked me out!'

'Did you go?'

'What d'you think? But I didn't tell me mam. She'd have had a fit. I were only fifteen. Anyway, I sneaked out when I could to meet him until the fair left town.'

'And?'

'Said he'd write.'

'And did he?'

'Did he 'eck. Oh, I had other boyfriends, don't get me wrong, but I was still hoping Denny would come back into me life. Then out of the blue came this birthday card.' She flicked a look at the Jess. 'I've still got it.' She took a breath and pushed her hair back. 'Anyway, the next year, when the fair came, I couldn't wait to see him. But he acted different towards me, stand-offish like. Then when I did manage to get him on his own he told me he were married. Broke me heart.' Janie stood up. 'Glass o' wine?'

'You sure?'

Janie nodded. 'I've been saving it for tonight.'

Again, Jess was surprised but said nothing. Left alone in the little garden she became aware of the rich colours of the sunset and the two donkeys plodding calmly about in the distance. Although Janie lived on next to nothing, her modest home held a natural beauty. Jess very rarely took the time to enjoy her surroundings – there was always so much to do indoors – but this evening, sitting here, she was forced to take notice of everything around her.

\*

Eddie took a beer from the fridge, turned on his favourite World Rally channel and sat back on the kitchen sofa. He rarely got a minute to himself these days, but he was determined to enjoy some down time. Eliot was sleeping soundly; the baby intercom was plugged in and the answerphone was turned on. He let out a self-satisfied sigh.

As he relaxed he began to recall a jumble of events, not least when Jess came back from her jaunts in Yorkshire with that toff Giles Morgan. Hoping to make a good impression, Eddie had spruced himself up, expecting to take her out to a restaurant and impress her, but Jess had surprised him when he went to pick her up. She had cooked him his favourite steak and kidney pie and they'd had a wonderful evening in her little flat. Part of him now yearned for those days and their new-found love. They were happy together and Eliot was a joy but to take some time out occasionally would be sweet.

Opening another can of beer he noticed how rough his hands had become. He found some hand cream by the sink and slathered it on. Restoring the Buick was hard graft but he was enjoying it. He fell to wondering what to do with her once she had reached peak condition. He needed to show her off, but how? Oh, there were plenty of classic car rallies where enthusiasts hung out to chat about their passion and parts for this and that, but he really needed something more. He scrolled through his phone and found a site that dealt with classic cars for the film industry. He had a sudden flash of insight – his name up there on the credits – *classic cars supplied by Eddie Gilbert*. Yeah, cool! Way to go.

His phone pinged; it was Mr Fairview, the guy who sold him the Buick. 'Hi Ed. How's it going?'

'Oh, hi mate. Yeah, all good. It's coming on a treat. I was wondering…'

\*

It was dark by the time Jess left Janie's cottage. Aided by the light from her phone she picked her way carefully along the unlit road. Now she understood the meaning of *black as night*. Without her phone she wouldn't be able to see a hand in front of her. It was disorientating but oddly comforting to look up and see a sky full of stars, although it made her feel very insignificant in the grand scheme of things. An owl hooted somewhere; she stood still to soak up the atmosphere, all her senses on high-alert. She thought it must be something to do with spending time with Janie. Jess had remarked on all the weird stuff she dabbled in but Janie had laughed it off, 'it were all that fortune teller's fault', but Jess had a feeling she would've taken the same path even without her introduction to Madam Rose.

Janie had asked Jess how she came to be living in the Dales, so she told her briefly about how she met Giles and how she thought he was her meal ticket to a better life. But Eddie had always been there for her, through thick and thin, especially when she was burgled. She told Janie about the letter from Shelley telling her they had come into money through their great grandfather's will and about their family history and how Giles had taken Jess to Yorkshire to explore more of her ancestry. But it had gradually dawned on her that Giles wasn't the person for her. It was Eddie she loved. This time it had been Janie's turn to look incredulous, saying it sounded like a fairy story. Jess had agreed. She still had to pinch herself sometimes.

Jess felt she knew Janie a little better now. She had been surprisingly open and told her all about her string of relationships after Denny but none of them had lasted very long. Then she'd met Rob who was into folk music and new-age living and thought that at last she'd found her soul mate. But he started knocking her about. It had taken immense courage to leave Rob but as soon as she was free of him Denny had turned up on her doorstep again. She had been prepared to give him one more chance but, true to form, he had waltzed out of her life again. Now all Janie's affections were lavished on her animals. They would never let her down.

The welcoming light from the windows of her beloved home and the fact that Eddie would be waiting for her gave Jess a warm glow. She hurried indoors, threw herself on Eddie, kissed him hungrily and took him upstairs. Eddie wasn't complaining; it was the perfect end to his evening.

# FIFTEEN

After a slow start things were picking up for Mandy and Trevor. Reece and Evie had totally fallen in love with their house and offered the full asking price. While the twins were at Carol's for a sleepover, they had cracked open a bottle of prosecco to celebrate and Trevor had cooked his special jerk chicken. Their euphoria had overflowed to the bedroom and they'd made love into the night.

Mandy had a break between clients so she quickly rang Jess to ask if they could come up for a couple of days, just the two of them. Carol had volunteered to have Kirsty and Keira leaving Mandy and Trevor free to do a recce on the properties they'd seen on *Rightmove*.

'Oh wow!' said Jess, 'Wicked! I'll have a look at the bookings but I'm sure we can squeeze you in somewhere. So they offered the full asking price?'

'Yeah, I can't believe it,' said Mandy, 'but they're mad about the house and they're such a lovely couple. She's about eight months pregnant.'

'Awesome!'

'I know, right? I'm sure they'll take care of it and love it as much as we have. I made them a cup of tea and we all sat in the garden which they adore. I just hope we can find what we want up in the Dales. Trevor's got his transfer and he needs to check it out, so we can kill two birds.'

'Fantastic!'

'Is this weekend OK?'

'Oh my God, I hope so.' She tapped away on her laptop. 'Yep, it's fine. You can have the front double but only for the weekend. It's really busy at the moment.'

'Phew! Thanks Jess. All I have to do now is hand in me notice.'

'Good luck!'

Mandy slipped her phone back in her pocket just as Liz poked her head round the staffroom door. She glared at Mandy. 'So, what's all this? Did I hear correctly?'

Mandy hung her head. 'Yeah, sorry. I was gonna tell you when I had a minute.'

Liz came in and slumped on one of the packing cases, something she never did. She hardly ever squeezed into this cupboard that doubled up as a staffroom. She preferred to stay in the salon where she could keep an eye on things. 'So, when are you going?'

'I'm not sure yet, but we've got a buyer and they want to move in as soon as possible.'

'I see.' Liz looked down at her hands. 'You're my best beautician, you know. I'll be sorry to lose you.'

This was a surprise. Liz was usually economical with her praise. Mandy had never had much to do with her anyway – working upstairs in the beauty salon while Liz worked downstairs – but now, up close, she noticed how tired and old she looked. 'I'm sorry.'

Liz took a breath. 'Yeah, well, can't be helped. You're probably doing the right thing. I don't know how much longer I can keep this place going to be honest.'

Mandy didn't want to dwell on that – she couldn't wait to move on. 'Trevor's got a transfer. We're going up to stay with Jess at the weekend.'

'Oh? How is she?'

Another surprise – Liz never gave Jess the time of day when she worked there. 'Yeah, she's good. She's happy with Eddie, got a fantastic B&B and tearoom business and her little boy is eight months old.'

Liz looked deflated. Mandy, it seemed, wasn't the only one at Top to Toe who felt left behind.

\*

As they sped up the motorway Mandy was looking forward to their weekend. Although Trevor had business to attend to and Jess would be busy in the tearoom during the day, she was hoping to get to know the surrounding area in preparation for when they moved. She was used to having everything on the doorstep in Peckham and assumed she would be wrenched out of her comfort zone in the Dales. She would likely need a car of her own too. But she was happy that her lovely home would be in the safe hands of Reece and Evie. They had been back to measure up for new curtains and to check that certain pieces of furniture would fit in and they were even more in love with the house. All that was left was for Mandy and Trevor to find their ideal home.

As they drove into the carpark, they noticed the double doors on Eddie's workshop were open. Trevor went to see him while Mandy stood drinking in the scene. The front tea garden was rammed with customers and dogs all enjoying their afternoon, candy-striped parasols providing much-needed shade. There were people out and about enjoying a walk or a bike ride along the river and Mandy filled up when she thought of how Jess's life had changed these past couple of years. As she walked through the gate, she noticed the back lawns were now scorched by the hot sun but the flower beds and tubs were still full of colour. Mandy smiled. Jess had turned into a proper little gardener. She remembered her remark two years ago – 'I've never even had a window box.'

Jess's face lit up when Mandy opened the back door. 'Mandy!' she flung her arms round her. 'You OK?'

'Yeah, I'm good. Trevor's with Eddie. I'm really looking forward to this. Oh, don't get me wrong, I love the twins to bits, but for the two of us to spend some quality time together...'

'Yeah, I know what you mean. Come and meet Janie. I'll get you some coffee in a tic.'

Mandy smiled at the thin woman with a strand of hair falling across her hot face. 'Hi. You look busy.'

Janie nodded and smiled at Jess. 'Look, if you wanna spend time with yer friends...'

Mandy felt in the way. 'It's all right. I'll take our stuff upstairs and get sorted. Which room did you say, Jess?'

'Number two, at the front, but first, go and get Trevor and I'll make you that coffee.'

From the doorway of the workshop Trevor pointed to the Buick. 'It's some car he's got in here. Come and have a look.'

Mandy tip-toed into the workshop trying to avoid the tools spread out on the floor.

Eddie pointed proudly to the car on the ramps. 'What d'you think?'

'Not being funny but, what is it?'

'A 1949 Buick, a classic American job.'

Mandy pulled a face.

'Yeah, I know it doesn't look much now, but you wait.'

She chuckled. 'If you say so. Jess has got the coffee on so don't be long.' She left them and went upstairs to unpack.

The last time Mandy and Trevor had stayed in the house Eliot had been a tiny baby and Jess had only just opened her B&B. Mandy assumed the little boy was now having his afternoon nap so she tried to be as quiet as possible. The view from the window drew her like a magnet. She gazed at the cloud shadows rolling over the hills and the sheep grazing in the distance. She hoped at least one of the properties tomorrow would come up to scratch.

Trevor crept up behind her, wrapped his arms round her and kissed the top of her head. 'Just think…all that could be on our doorstep too.'

'Oh, I do hope so Trev. What will we do if we don't like any of the houses tomorrow?'

'We'll just have to keep looking.'

Mandy's face crumpled. 'I know. But…I don't want us to live apart.'

'It might not come to that. Think positive, yeah?' She gave him a beaming smile. 'That's better. Now, come on, let's grab that coffee, I'm gasping.'

In the conservatory two frothy coffees and a plate of fresh scones with jam and clotted cream awaited them on the coffee table.

'What's she like?' said Mandy. 'I didn't expect all this.' But she wasted no time in getting stuck in.

Jess poked her head round the door, 'All right? I thought you'd be hungry.'

Mandy nodded, her mouth full.

'Yeah, thanks Jess,' said Trevor, 'they'll go down a treat, but where's Eddie? I thought he'd be in.'

'Huh, swear to God, it's a wonder he doesn't sleep in there with that thing. At least I've got Janie to help me.'

'So what's the story there, then?' whispered Mandy, wiping a blob of cream off her chin.

Jess turned to see that she was needed in the kitchen. 'Tell you later.'

*

Laura closed the door to her room and went downstairs. It had been an exhausting journey, queues on the motorway with roadworks for miles and she'd flopped onto the sumptuous bed as soon as she'd arrived at Bracken Farmhouse. However, it had been a relief not to have to listen to Roger's moans today. She hadn't told him what she was doing either, only that she fancied getting away for a few days. After days of silence, he had given her the third degree. 'But why? We've only just come back from there.' And, 'I didn't think you were overly impressed with that place?' But she had stood her ground and told him it was *he* who wasn't impressed and that it was something she felt compelled to do. She wasn't going to be talked round anymore. Her mother was right – she needed her own life.

Bracken Farmhouse was even better than she remembered, or rather, she saw it through her own eyes instead of Roger's distorted view. Her room was of a very high standard. She'd stayed in some top-notch places in her time and this one would certainly be up there with the best. Jess had told her that, although she didn't provide evening meals, the Green Man had an extensive menu and it was within walking distance. Laura was thankful as it meant she wouldn't need to get back in the car. She had booked a table for 7pm, early for her, but she'd only had a cereal bar since her coffee and cake at the busy motorway services this morning.

She decided to stretch her legs before dinner and get some idea of what the village had to offer. Strolling along the river, a few hikers passed her with a 'Good evening.' She filled her lungs with the clean air as she made her way over the ancient foot bridge stopping to watch the tiny fish swimming in and out of the weed in the crystal-clear water below. Standing on the far bank she had a good view of the village. A little way along from the Green Man stood a row of terraced cottages. A large tabby cat sat by the one at the far end licking his paws and washing his face. She remembered her granny telling her, 'If a cat washes over its ears it means it's going to rain.' She hoped it was only an old wives' tale – she wanted to enjoy her few days away in sunshine. She assumed the building a few yards further on from the cottages was the village hall and beyond that were a general store and a bakery. On the nearside was a high brick wall; probably some stately pile lay behind, thought Laura, and beyond that she could just make out the church spire through some tall trees. At the far end of the road, along from the general store, there was what looked like an empty shop. Her interest piqued, she crossed back over the bridge and went to investigate.

The shop was small but it looked as if there was a flat above. This would be ideal for she needed somewhere to live as well as business premises. The navy-blue paintwork was cracked and peeling. The shop window had a huge crack in it and behind the glass a faded blue blind obscured her view of the inside. To the left of the window a half-glazed door displayed a closed sign and another dusty blind. Laura wondered how long it had been empty and who it belonged to. There was nothing to tell her. Although it needed a lot of work the shop was in a prime position for her little enterprise; she felt sure there would be plenty of passing trade. Her imagination galloped ahead and a rush of excitement prickled her skin.

\*

After dinner, while Trevor was meeting his future staff at the supermarket and Eliot had been put to bed, Jess, Eddie and Mandy took their ice-cold drinks into the garden. Strings of fairy lights adorned the pergola; the golden sun was slipping slowly towards the horizon and the scent of freshly mown grass filled Mandy's senses. She was in heaven. She took out her phone and showed Jess the houses they were going to view tomorrow.

'Oh my God, that's gorgeous!' said Jess, scanning the one Mandy liked best. 'I can see you living there.'

'Is it far from here?'

Jess shook her head. 'It's the next village. I can't wait to have you living up here.'

'Yeah,' said Eddie. 'Let's hope the job measures up.' But he was half hoping it wouldn't and that Trevor could work for him and Jess, keeping an eye on the accounts. Maybe Property Manager would sound an attractive job title. This would allow Eddie to work on his precious Buick, one of the many classic cars he hoped to transform. After Eddie's last conversation with Mr Fairview there was no reason why he couldn't turn his hobby into a thriving business. Also, if Trevor was their property manager it would also mean Jess could spend more time with Eliot.

Trevor's wheels crunched on the gravel and Mandy was instantly on her feet. Jess and Eddie held up crossed fingers and hopeful faces. Trevor came through the gate with a confident swagger and a thumbs-up. Mandy threw her arms round him.

'Awesome!' said Jess. 'All it leaves now is to find your perfect house tomorrow.'

\*

Carol had taken the twins over the park as the weather was too nice to be stuck indoors. She had pushed them on the swings to their shouts of 'Higher, higher!' and she'd bought them ice creams and sat on a bench to watch them at play. They had grown into two delightful little girls. Oh, they had their moments, they weren't all sweetness and light, no children were, but she congratulated herself on having some input in their upbringing. She loved being a grandma and doing all the activities with Kirsty and Keira that grandmas do like reading them stories at bedtime, cutting and sticking and baking buns. She enjoyed meeting the twins from school and chatting to the other mums at the gate and, in the school holidays, taking Kirsty and Keira out for the day. But she knew, in a few years' time, they would join the ranks of other teenagers hooked on smart phones and iPads and evenings with Grandma would gradually fade away to be replaced by sleepovers with friends. No matter how she looked at it, she was going to miss them when they moved. Carol was secretly hoping that Trevor wouldn't take the job or they wouldn't be able to find their ideal property. But looking at it logically and trying to be altruistic she knew it would be the best thing for them. She knew they would leave Peckham one day in any case.

Carol hadn't wanted to leave Kent when she married Barry but his work was in Peckham and so was his family. She couldn't get used to their different ways at first; it was like living in another country. Barry had called her Posh Bird when they started going out but when they got married she was forced to get used to a different way of life, shopping in Rye Lane instead of the more select places like Tonbridge and Canterbury. And now her darling daughter would have to adjust to a different way of life, albeit one that she wanted and not one that was thrust upon her.

Once they'd got on their feet, Carol had wanted Barry to buy their own house in a more salubrious area, but it had never happened. Barry hadn't wanted to be saddled with a mortgage round his neck, so she had made the best of the council flat they had been allotted. She had longed for a garden, but Barry's logic dictated that she didn't need a garden when she had the whole of Peckham Rye in which to roam around. He had never understood why she wanted to nurture her own plants and design her own garden. Instead, she had made do with a window box on the balcony, filling it with colour, until she and Barry were rehoused years later in the house on Goose Green. That's why she was over the moon for Mandy and Trevor when they bought their house on Peckham Rye. Carol had loved watching her daughter turn the neglected back yard into the flourishing paradise that it was today.

The twins came running up to her and she ached with love for them. Yes, she was going to miss them all dreadfully.

# SIXTEEN

Jess was spending some much-needed time with Eliot in the conservatory, Eddie was on breakfast duty and Janie, who had breezed in bright and early, was serving. Everything was jogging along nicely until Kate poked her nose in and glared at Janie. 'For heaven's sake, what are you doing? Give it here!' She pulled the tray away from her and began to rearrange the cups and plates. 'There, like that.'

Janie didn't want to make a fuss but she also didn't want to stand by and let Kate bully her. 'Sorry, but Jess likes it done like *this*.' Janie pulled the tray back again and some of the coffee slopped into the saucer.

'Now look what you've done, you stupid cow!'

Eddie turned from the Aga. 'All right there, Kate?'

'I was just telling her the best way to arrange a tray.'

Eddie frowned, incredulous. 'What?'

'Oh, nothing, just something I noticed. It'll keep.' She took her mop and bucket and went to do the necessary.

Janie shook her head and rolled her eyes at Eddie, poured another cup of coffee and took her tray into the tearoom.

Mandy had heard the exchange. She looked round at Janie. 'You OK?'

'Aye, I'm fine thanks.' She went back in the kitchen for Mandy and Trevor's cooked breakfast and placed it in front of them, pasted a smile on her face, asked the other guests if there was anything else they needed and took some dirty pots back to the kitchen.

'Did you hear that?' Mandy asked Trevor. 'It sounded like Kate was having a dig at Janie. She doesn't deserve it. She works well enough and she's always got a smile.'

Trevor lifted an eyebrow. 'I'd stay out of it if I was you, love. Jess will sort it.'

'But that's just it. Kate always chooses her moments when Jess isn't around.'

Back in the kitchen, Eddie asked Janie, 'What was Kate on about?'

'She wants me to do things *her* way. I told her I do it like Jess wants.'

Eddie had a good idea what was happening. From what he'd seen of Kate she was a fly in the proverbial. He hated the way she barged in and kept having a go at Janie. 'Is everyone sorted now?'

Janie nodded, 'Just got another pot of tea and two more coffees to take in and I think that's the lot,' she said, filling the cups. 'Oh, and your friends might want some more toast or another drink. I'll go and check.'

Eddie watched her. There was nothing wrong with Janie or the way she worked. He would like to dismiss Kate but it wasn't down to him. However, Jess needed to know what was going on in here this morning.

*

As they drove out of the car park, Mandy sat hugging the house details and crossed her fingers.

'I don't know about that first one,' said Trevor. 'It's in a fantastic location, views for miles and only a fraction of the price of ours, but it needs of lot of work.'

Mandy wasn't sure either. 'I know but it would mean we could pay off our mortgage, Trev.'

'Yeah, and that's a very attractive thought!'

The sat nav directed them down a little country lane that looked like an unused farm track, grass growing down the centre and tall cow parsley on both sides. It was only wide enough for one car and Trevor hoped they wouldn't meet another one coming the other way; there was no passing place. But they came to the end without a hitch and there before them was the property standing in its own grounds. It looked smaller and more forlorn than it did on *Rightmove*.

Trevor's expression reflected Mandy's thoughts. 'Well, let's have a look now we're here.'

They walked up the uneven path to the weather-beaten front door and knocked. A little while later they heard someone shuffling round from the side entrance. An elderly man stood before them in stained jogging bottoms and a better-days jumper.

Mandy approached him and held out her hand. 'Mr Gravely? Mr and Mrs King.'

He squinted at them. 'You here for the viewing?'

'Yes, that's right.'

He looked Trevor up and down. 'Huh, I suppose you'd better come in.' He shuffled back the way he'd come, through the back door and into a dark kitchen.

'Right, I'll let you look round if you don't mind, only I'm a bit dodgy on me feet since the stroke.' He tottered through to the sitting room, sat heavily in an armchair and picked up his newspaper.

Mandy felt sorry for him, but she didn't want to start a lengthy conversation about his health. They had a lot to get through this morning. She scanned the small dark kitchen – the deep sink chipped and tea-stained, some dried-up household soap sat in a dish and a shabby curtain skirted beneath. The electric cooker was a museum piece and the lino was worn through. Mandy screwed up her face and whispered, 'Really?'

Trevor nodded. 'Yeah but think what it could be. It's in a lovely spot...we could knock the wall down and put a new kitchen in...'

...'Sorry, Trev, I don't think I can do this.'

'Listen,' whispered Trevor, 'it could be a fantastic project. We'd have enough money to gut the place and get an architect in…'

Mandy shook her head vehemently. 'No, Trev, not with the twins.'

'We could rent somewhere while we do it up…'

She turned away and walked into the sitting room. Trevor followed.

Mr Gravely looked over the top of his newspaper. 'Don't mind me.'

Mandy cast a quick glance over the room and saw what looked like some water marks halfway up the wall. Peering out of the metal-framed window she noticed the river was about thirty feet away. When they first got the details of this house, she thought how lovely it would be to live near a river, but now she wasn't so sure. Even if they did decide to buy it and refurbish it, would it be worth the flood risk?

The smell of damp plaster hit them as they went upstairs. The bedrooms were smaller than they'd been led to believe and the bathroom was out of the ark with a high-level toilet cistern and a chain.

Mandy shook her head. 'Look Trev, I know we can get this for a song, but it needs bull-dozing and starting from scratch. I'm surprised it's not put up for auction. I can't do it.'

'OK, I suppose you're right, but it was worth a look.'

They went downstairs to find Mr Gravely.

'I'm sorry,' said Trevor, 'but it's a bit small for us.'

Mr Gravely remained seated. 'That's all right, lad. Can you see yourselves out?'

Trevor closed the door behind them and stood gazing at the countryside. 'Shame, it's in a lovely spot.'

'I know and it's all very sad. The poor man must've lived here for years.'

Trevor tried again. 'Don't you feel you could love it, just a little?' He turned to see Mandy was already in the car.

The next property was a three-bed detached, recently built, but they were disappointed to find it was on a large estate. After driving down a warren of narrow roads they came to the house with the For Sale board outside.

Trevor looked at his watch. 'We're early. D'you wanna have a walk round, get a feel for the place, or shall we not bother?'

Mandy's heart sank. 'I can't see us living here, Trev. The whole point of moving up here is to have a view or at least a bigger garden. Let's go.'

The last house was looking more hopeful, in a prime position with views. According to the estate agent's details the village had an active community, a shop and a pub but the school was a bus ride away.

A young couple showed them in. 'Hi, I'm Kathy and this is Nathan.'

Mandy and Trevor were agog. The house was obviously well loved; it was immaculate inside. The kitchen was newly refurbished and the lounge was double aspect. There was even a separate annexe that would be perfect for Carol *if* she decided to come and live with them. It was all looking too good to be true.

When they had seen the whole property, Kathy asked if they would like a cup of tea.

'That would be lovely,' said Mandy, thinking breakfast was a long time ago.

'A shame it's come on to rain,' said Kathy, 'otherwise we could've sat in the garden.'

The garden! Mandy had forgotten to look out there. Through the kitchen window the garden didn't look much bigger than hers which was disappointing. But the views were to die for and she wondered if a bigger garden was all that important when they had all this on the doorstep. 'So,' said Mandy, 'what's your position? Have you found somewhere?'

Nathan flicked a glance at his wife, 'The one we want's in a chain…'

'What about yourselves?' asked Kathy.

'We've sold,' said Trevor, 'and they want to move in as soon as possible.'

Mandy bit her lip thinking of all the months she would be living without Trevor while they waited with baited breath. It was all going so well until now.

# SEVENTEEN

Rudolf Pemberton-Jones lit the last of his Davidoff cigars and puffed on it. Rosemary was out with her cronies at some barbeque or other leaving him to fend for himself yet again. He didn't care for barbeques, all those burgers and sausages and weird-looking salads, they always gave him indigestion. However, being left alone had its benefits. Rosemary hated him smoking indoors and always looked down her long nose if he had more than one glass of whisky. Ha! While the cat's away… He went to his sadly depleted drinks cabinet and poured himself a large glass of single malt, the perfect partner to his cigar and his only two remaining luxuries. Sitting in his armchair he let his mind drift. He'd go and see what was on offer food-wise in a minute. Gone were the days of the cook who would rustle up his favourite steak in red wine, or a pheasant or two after a days' shooting. He salivated at the thought, downed his whisky and poured another.

He unlocked the French windows to waft out the cigar smoke and another piece of the frame fell off. The whole damn place was falling down round his ears. Standing on the terrace, master of all he surveyed, his heart plummeted. He'd had to get rid of his one remaining gardener and he hated doing it himself. Rosemary was always too busy, what with the WI, the parish council and what-not. He dreaded to think what the once magnificent gardens would look like in a few years' time.

Before the house had dilapidated to this extent, Rosemary had wanted them to open the house to the public, but he hadn't wanted the riff-raff with their snotty-nosed kids traipsing through his property. No, he preferred to squeeze the money out of his few remaining tenants but even that was proving more difficult of late. When his father died and left him the estate Rudolf hadn't realised how bad things were. This house had been in the family for centuries, but each subsequent custodian had barely held onto it by their fingernails. It all came down to living within one's means of course but none of them had been any good at that, what with extravagant masked balls, jazz parties and the like. Now, all that was left were the echoes of grander times, the whole estate forgotten like the churchyard next door. That was another bone of contention. The vicar was long gone and the local synod had sold off the medieval church. It was apparently now a retreat for bible-bashers – probably a foil for some weird cult, thought Rudolf, as he drained his glass. Was nothing sacred anymore?

\*

Trevor had suggested they all go out for a meal tonight, so he'd booked a table at the Green Man for 8pm. Jess didn't think it was fair on Eliot to be dragged away from his cot again so she'd reluctantly asked Kate to babysit. She didn't think it fair to drag Janie back in after working in the tearoom all day.

The Green Man was buzzing with convivial chatter and the sounds of people enjoying a delicious meal. Mandy's eyes were everywhere – she'd never seen a pub like it – wood carvings, wizards and witches crammed into every nook and cranny and all weird and wonderful things hung from the rafters. She was so engrossed that she hadn't realised the others were sitting at a table. She went to join them.

Greg had given them some menus and Trevor had ordered a bottle of sauvignon blanc and a jug of iced water.

Jess read the specials board. 'Minted lamb cutlets with sauté potatoes on a bed of spinach and pine nuts, pork belly with roasted vegetables, traditional beer-battered cod and fat chips, fish pie or mushroom stroganoff. Oh my God! I need a minute to think.'

'Well,' said Eddie, 'I know what I'm having; its ages since I've had proper fish and chips.'

Trevor scanned the board and then his menu again. 'Oh, man, so much choice!'

'Yeah,' said Jess, 'I know what you mean but I think I'll have the pork.'

'Well, I'm having the lamb cutlets,' said Mandy and put her menu down.

They all stared at Trevor.

'Come on Trev,' said Mandy, 'hurry up I'm starving!'

'D'you know what? I've never had fish pie. Let's go with that.'

'You won't be disappointed,' came a voice from behind him.

Trevor turned to see a woman sitting on her own with an empty plate. 'Oh right, thanks.'

Greg returned with their wine and started to pour whilst taking their orders, 'Great choices, guys. Be about thirty minutes, OK?'

Jess grimaced. 'Really?'

'Yeah, sorry, cook's flat-out. I'll bring a selection of nibbles.'

'Thanks Greg, you're a star.' Jess took a sip of wine and turned to Mandy. 'So, what d'you think you'll do? About the house, I mean?'

Mandy blew out a long sigh. 'I dunno. I really liked the one with the annexe. Trouble is it could take months and I don't fancy living at mum's all that time. And Trevor will have to find somewhere to live.'

Trevor picked up her hand, kissed it. 'we'll keep looking, yeah?'

'You don't fancy the project, then?' asked Jess.

'Nope, end of,' said Mandy.

'It could be fun,' said Trevor.

Mandy gave him one of her looks.

Jess wished she hadn't brought it up. She didn't want a damper on the evening. 'Well, you're not screwed yet. Early days, something'll turn up, you'll see.'

Greg brought them a selection of breads with olives, balsamic vinegar and olive oil. Trevor topped up their glasses and they dived in then a sudden crack of thunder had them all looking at each other.

'I don't think it'll be much,' said Eddie, stabbing an olive, 'it wasn't forecast.'

'I hope you're right,' said Jess, 'none of us has a coat or a brolly.'

A flash of lightning lit up the bar and thunder cracked overhead. The woman sitting behind Trevor jumped up and went to pay her bill.

Jess recognised her, it was Mrs Dean. 'It's OK. Kate's there if she needs anything.'

Another crack of thunder and the lights went out sending a collective moan reverberating around the bar.

Greg emerged. 'Hey guys, listen up. We're doing our best to get everyone's food out but it's not looking good. Just bear with us, OK?'

'Oh bugger!' said Jess, 'Why now? I was really looking forward to this.'

Mandy squeezed her hand. 'So was I.'

'No sweat,' said Eddie, 'if the worst comes to the worst at least we've got the Aga.'

As soon as Kate had been confident Jess and Eddie and friends were well out of sight and Eliot was fast asleep, she'd wasted no time in opening Jess's laptop that she'd left in the kitchen. Kate had tried all the likely names and combinations she could think of for the password, but none were accepted. Feeling defeated, she'd made a cup of tea and taken it into the lounge, the room that was generally out of bounds. She was rarely asked to clean in here so she grabbed the opportunity to have a nose around. Settling into the sumptuous sofa, her gaze fell on the large oil painting above the fireplace. She wasn't into art – she couldn't see what all the fuss was about – but she assumed this was the one that Mrs Morgan had been on about. Kate smiled smugly as she remembered being one of the exceptional cleaning team for the Greenwich agency. Yes, Mrs Morgan had been very pleased with her work, so much so that she had taken Kate into her confidence and told her all about the history of the painting.

As she sank further back in the cushions, Kate spied another laptop perched on the desk by the window. What a gift! She jumped up to take a look, moved the mouse pad and, hey presto, the accounts page for Bracken Farmhouse sprang into life. Yes! The adrenalin coursed through her veins as she tapped away at the keyboard. No time to lose. However, just as she was about to take a closer look another clap of thunder turned the screen black. 'Shit!'

The front door slammed, and Kate jumped up. Her heart pounding, she opened the lounge door a crack and caught sight of a woman disappearing at the top of the stairs. Phew! Thank God it wasn't Jess, Eddie et al but she knew it wouldn't be long before they came back.

Kate hurried to the kitchen, rummaged around in the dresser for some candles, set them on the table and lit them. Perching on the kitchen sofa with a magazine, she took some deep breaths and tried to look as if she'd been sitting there all evening. Not before time. She heard voices and the sound of a key in the door.

'I hope you didn't mind,' started Kate, 'but I took the liberty of lighting some candles. Did you have a nice meal?'

Jess took a towel to her hair. 'No, we never got that far. Bloody power cut! Eliot OK?'

Kate nodded. 'Not a murmur.'

'Great, thanks Kate.'

'Wanna lift back?' asked Eddie.

'No, it's all right, I'll ring Mike,' said Kate.

'You sure?'

'You've been drinking, anyway,' Jess reminded him.

'That's true.'

Jess began to organise some food and Eddie opened a bottle of wine while Trevor and Mandy took themselves upstairs to dry off.

Kate flew out of the kitchen, took out her mobile and rang Mike. She suddenly had a nasty feeling she'd forgotten to close the laptop. She started pacing the hallway. Did she or didn't she? She couldn't remember. Should she go back and check? No, Jess's friends were on their way downstairs. What if they went in there? No, she couldn't risk it. She heard Mike's car on the gravel. 'Bye Jess,' she called out.

'Yeah, bye Kate,' came the reply.

The Aga was a godsend and as Jess and Eddie, Mandy and Trevor sat down to eat by candlelight, the distant rumbles of thunder and the gentle patter on the windows meant the storm was gradually moving away.

Eddie stabbed a sausage and held it up. 'Bit early for breakfast!'

'OK by me,' said Trevor, 'I can always eat a fry-up.'

Although it wasn't her original choice, Mandy was thankful for the food on her plate. Although their meal in Green Man had been interrupted she was enjoying her evening and was looking forward to many more like it. If only they could find their forever home.

'Are you going to look again tomorrow?' asked Jess. 'I know it's Sunday but you could at least suss out some of the other villages.'

'We've only got the morning,' said Mandy. 'We've both got work on Monday.'

'That's the trouble,' said Trevor, 'never enough time. I need to look for a place to rent, too, so I'll have somewhere to live when I start the new job.'

'I'll have a look at the bookings later,' said Jess. 'The Cow Shed might be an option but we're coming into high season now.'

'Thanks Jess.' Mandy crossed her fingers under the table. Living in the Cow Shed with Trevor and the twins during the summer holidays would be far from a hardship. Also, with the pressure taken off, they could take their time and be more likely to find the house of their dreams. She drained her wineglass and stood up. 'Well, I don't know about you Trev, but I'm bushed. I think I'll turn in.'

'Not a bad idea,' said Trevor.

Mandy suddenly felt awkward. 'You OK Jess, or do you want help with clearing this lot away?'

Jess shook her head. 'You go, we'll do it later.'

When they had gone upstairs, Eddie and Jess took their wine into the lounge. As he sat down he noticed his laptop was open. 'Funny, I thought I shut that down. Was it you?'

Jess tucked her feet up and shook her head. 'Nope, not guilty.'

Eddie walked over and frowned at the screen. 'That's odd.'

'What is?' Jess flew to his side. 'Oh my God.'

'I dunno but I think we'll have to keep this door locked when we're out in future.' Eddie looked in the desk drawers but it didn't look as if anything had been disturbed. He scrolled through the documents on his laptop and let out a sigh. As far as he could make out nothing had changed since the last time he'd logged on but he couldn't remember leaving all those windows open. He logged off and closed it down.

'Bloody Kate!' shouted Jess. 'Swear to God that woman's a nightmare.'

'Yeah, you're right, but let's give her the benefit of the doubt for now.'

Jess thought he was being too lenient. She noticed Kate's favourite mug sitting comfortably next to Eddie's laptop.

*

Rosemary Pemberton-Jones came home to find her husband sprawled on the chesterfield in a drunken stupor, the French windows flung wide and the floor sopping wet. She slammed the French windows. He didn't stir. She had a good mind to leave him there; it wouldn't be the first time.

She'd had a lovely evening at the barbeque until the rain sent them all running for cover but even then, they'd continued their evening indoors by candlelight. It had been such a refreshing change from listening to Rudolf bleating on about the lack of money while he disappeared into a bottle. Being with like-minded people had allowed her to forget how bad things were but the sight of Rudolf, in another one of his self-pitying torpors, brought her down to earth. He'd had nothing to eat either – the kitchen was still how she'd left it and the ham salad she'd made him was in the fridge. It was all very depressing.

Janie, on the other hand, had had a lovely evening. When she'd felt the storm coming, she had quickly run indoors to prepare some of her oils, incense sticks and candles. She had read about storm magic – it was powerful and energising and she'd been eager to put it to the test. Jess and Eddie were good to her and she wanted to give something back.

Standing by the open door, Janie had breathed in the storm-charged atmosphere, her pulse racing. Gandalf had felt it too, eyes alert, ears twitching as he sat by her feet. While the fork lightening split the night sky and the thunder cracked overhead, Janie had stepped out into the deluge and thrown back her head to feel the full force of rain on her face. Thrusting up her hands to the heavens she had uttered her incantation.

# EIGHTEEN

Laura had found a few shops on the internet that looked possible for her business and, although today was Sunday, she was determined to drive out and take a look at them after breakfast.

She was the first and only guest in Jessica's Parlour. After choosing some fruit juice and cereal she took a seat by the window. Eddie was surprised to see her at this hour.

'You're up bright and early! Coffee?'

'Please.'

'Any cooked food?'

Laura looked at the menu. 'I see you have eggs benedict?'

'Yeah, going down a storm at the minute. One or two muffins?'

'Mm, two please.'

'Coming right up.'

Laura took out her phone again to study the shops on her list. It had been a long time since she'd felt a thrill like this. She couldn't think why she hadn't done it before. All these years spent pandering to Roger's likes and dislikes – mainly the latter – when she could've been enjoying her independence. Although there were a couple of shops that required little or no alteration, the little long-forgotten shop in the village was crying out to be loved. If only she could find out owned it.

Eddie came back with her coffee. 'Were you in the Green Man last night?'

Laura nodded. 'And what a delightful place it is. The food is excellent. If it hadn't been for the storm I would've stayed longer.'

'Yeah, pity about that.'

'Leadale is a lovely village. I had a nice walk along by the river yesterday and noticed an empty shop at the far end of the road. I don't suppose you know who owns it? Only I'm looking for business premises.'

'I've got a feeling that's ol' PJ. Hang on, I'll go and ask Jess.'

Laura breathed in the delicious aroma of the coffee as a shaft of sunlight fell across her table. She had a good feeling about today. But who was this PJ, she wondered.

Eddie placed the eggs benedict in front of her. 'There we are, enjoy! Oh, by the way, that old shop, PJ does own it.'

Laura frowned, curious.

'Sorry, Mr Pemberton-Jones.' He put a scrap of paper in front of her. 'His wife's on the parish council.'

Laura's eyes lit up. 'Excellent! Thank you so much.'

'No worries.'

In the kitchen, Jess looked round from feeding Eliot. 'What did she say?'

Eddie put on a posh voice. 'Excellent, thank you so much! Ha, I wonder what she wants it for?'

Jess stuffed another spoonful of cereal into Eliot's open mouth and shrugged. 'Sounds like she's out of her depth up here and God knows how long that shop's been empty; must be gross inside.'

'Yeah, and no doubt he'll want an arm and two legs for the rent.'

'I hope she knows what she's getting into – the PJs are a nightmare to deal with. ' Jess let Eliot feed himself the last two mouthfuls, wiped his face and hands and put him in his walker. Remembering what she'd had to sort out when she bought Bracken Farmhouse, she wondered if she could be of help to Mrs Dean. She went to ask her.

'Everything OK?'

'Yes, lovely thank you,' said Laura.

'Can I get you anything else, more coffee, toast?'

Laura shook her head and stood up. 'I need to get going – got a lot to do today.'

'OK. If you want any help, you know, with anything else? Only I know what it's like…I had a lot to sort out when I bought this place.'

'That's very kind, thank you.'

'You're welcome.'

Jess went back to the kitchen to find that Eddie had disappeared, and Eliot was getting hooked up in the toys on the floor, the wheels of his walker about to decapitate his teddy.

Jess chuckled. 'What're you like?'

Eliot gurgled happily, bounced his toes on the floor and held up his arms to her. She picked him up and cuddled him, breathed in his baby scent.

Eddie was back in his workshop. The Buick was looking more like the picture he had in his head but there was still a lot of work to do. Luckily Jess didn't know how much money he'd thrown at it but at least it had come out of his own pocket. He'd taken delivery of two new chrome bumpers the other day and they sat on an old carpet waiting to be put on. But the hood was past it; he needed a new one and that meant megabucks. He hadn't told Jess what he planned to use the Buick for, but Mr Fairview had been very helpful on the subject of using the Buick for the film industry. Eddie's mind travelled off into the realms of greatness every time he thought about it. He intended to buy another classic car once he'd got this one under his belt and, in the future, to have a string of them, once he'd got his foot in the door.

While Trevor was eating his breakfast, he wondered if he and Mandy should spend the day in the Dales and travel back later tonight. They had searched the internet again and had come up with a few more houses they liked but they really needed to see them in the flesh. Although it was

Sunday and the estate agents would be closed, they could at least get a feel for the locations.

Mandy looked up from her plate. 'Why don't we spend the day up here and go back tonight? Mum won't mind having the twins a bit longer.'

Trevor stopped chewing, eyes wide. 'You're good at that.'

'What?'

'Reading my mind.'

Mandy's heart leapt. She quickly finished her breakfast and went to tell Jess.

'Awesome! Maybe you'll have more luck today.'

'Yeah, I hope so. Did you have a look at the bookings?'

'Yeah sorry,' she screwed up her nose, 'the Cow Shed's fully booked right through to the end of August. I've looked at all the options but the whole place is booked apart from a few odd days here and there.'

Mandy sighed. 'Well, I'm pleased for you but it doesn't help us!' Trevor was jangling his car keys. 'Look, don't worry. Something will turn up. We'll see you later.'

'Yeah, good luck.'

There was a tap on the back door and Sam popped his head in.

Jess smiled at him. 'Hi Sam. Got your days mixed up?'

He shook his head. 'No lass, I've still got all me marbles. Just thought I'd give me da's old bike a bit of a work-out like.'

'Oh, right. I've got a minute if you wanna cuppa?'

'Aye, that would be grand.' He removed his bicycle clips and sat at the table. He watched Jess while she worked. 'Seems a bit quiet in 'ere this morning. Where's Eddie and the little fella?'

'Eliot's over there,' she pointed to the little boy quietly playing with his toys at the other end of the kitchen, 'and I'll give you three guesses where Eddie is.'

Sam smiled and shot his eyes skywards.

Jess set his mug of tea on the table and made herself a coffee. Was it her imagination or did he look a bit edgy? 'So, what's the real reason you're here then, Sam?'

Sam gave a wry smile; there were no flies on Jess. 'I don't say much as yer know but I do notice things. I've been meaning to have a word. I don't like how Kate rips into poor Janie. There's nowt wrong with Janie.'

'I know, I don't like it either, but I don't want to lose Kate, she's a good worker.'

'That might be, but I wouldn't ignore it if I were you.'

Jess took a sip of coffee and looked at Sam. She sensed there was more to come.

Sam gazed into his mug and ran a finger down the handle. 'Did you know Kate's Auntie Ivy used to run the post office?'

'No, I didn't. But I thought Kate and her husband moved up here when he retired?'

'Aye they did but Kate used to live here before she got married. She didn't want to leave but her husband was a Londoner and his job was down there. I think he worked in technology or summat.'

Jess nodded. 'And what did Kate do? For work, I mean.'

'She didn't need to work, he earned good money, but I think she looked after wealthy people's houses and the like for a bit o' pin money.' He drained his mug and continued, 'Auntie Ivy was the village gossip, always had her ears pricked up and her fingers in t' pies. Something in the blood, you might say.'

'Yeah, I get it.' Jess was putting two and two together.

'Anyway, when Auntie Ivy died she left her cottage to Kate. Ivy had never married and she didn't have anyone else to leave it to. Well, Kate wasted no time; as soon as her husband retired she was up here like a shot.'

\*

Lydia Morgan was fuming. It wasn't good enough. She thought she had the measure of Katherine when she'd been looking after her Greenwich apartment, but maybe she'd misread her. If it wasn't for her design consultancy business, here in France, Lydia decided, she would be putting a stop to the Blonde Tart's little venture in person.

Lydia stared out the window of her apartment down on the little town square bathed in bright sunlight – stylish people enjoying their day in the market, buying delicious produce, fine wines and cheeses – so different to dull old England. She was dying to get even with her so-called distant cousin who had done her out of her great-grandfather's will. She was still questioning the legality of the Tart's heritage and that of her meddling sister. Giles was to blame of course – if it hadn't been for him and his father delving into things that didn't concern them, she wouldn't be in this position. And, on top of all that, Giles had seen fit to give that Tart her painting of Coverdale! How dare he, it wasn't his to give! She would have to work on that too. If Katherine wasn't up to the task then she would either have to find someone else or do it herself. A wicked smile slid over her face – she had a good mind to book a flight – she hadn't had any fun in ages.

# NINETEEN

Early Monday morning there was tap at the back door. It was too early for Sam or the other deliveries.

'I'll get it,' said Jess.

It was Ramona with her daughter in the buggy. 'Hi Jess. I don't know if you fancy it but we're starting up a new toddler group, taking it in turns in each other's houses. The thing is the parish council have put the fees up on the village hall and we don't think it's fair.'

'Oh, right, come in. You'll have to excuse the mess.'

Ramona lifted her daughter out of the buggy. She was off like a shot to see what toys she could play with.

'We can sit in the conservatory,' said Jess, following the little girl. She straightened up the cushions on the rattan sofa and moved the toys to one side. 'Coffee?'

'Ooh, d'you know what? I'd kill for a cappuccino! One sugar.' Ramona's eyes were everywhere. 'Wow! Some place you got here.'

'Thanks.' Jess went back to the kitchen for the coffee.

Eddie was on breakfast duty. 'Who's that?'

'Ramona from Toddlers. You OK for a minute?'

'Yeah, I'm cool.'

Jess placed Ramona's coffee in front of her.

'Ooh, lovely.' Ramona watched Eliot playing on the floor. 'He looks a lot happier today.'

'Yeah, thank God. I didn't wanna run off like that but I was worried about him. Then someone suggested he might have meningitis and I freaked!'

'Yeah, I bet.'

'Anyway, he's fine.'

Eliot grinned at Ramona.

'Aw, look! He's got another tooth, bless him.' She glanced at her daughter. 'Poppy! Put that down and come and say hello to Eliot.'

Jess resolved to put her baking on hold and hoped Eddie wouldn't slope off back to his workshop. It was lovely to see Ramona and Poppy who was now amusing Eliot, his happy little voice echoing around the conservatory.

Jess sniffed the air, 'Oh my God!' and ran to the kitchen just in time to rescue a batch of cherry scones from the oven. Eddie had obviously nipped out while her back was turned. She put a couple on a plate with some butter and took them into the conservatory.

Ramona's eyes were on stalks. 'Oh wow! You are clever Jess. I was never any good at bakin'.' She grabbed a scone and buttered it, took a bite. 'Mmm, lovely.'

'So,' said Jess, 'where do you live?'

Ramona forced down a lump of scone. 'Mm, on the new estate, up behind the hall. This is delish! I haven't had any breakfast.'

Jess frowned. 'I didn't know there were any houses behind the village hall?'

'No! Not there, the butt-ugly mansion the other side of the road.'

'PJ's place?'

Ramona nodded, her mouth full.

Jess grinned. 'You're not from around here, are you?'

Ramona shook her head. 'Nope, we moved up from London three years ago.' She looked at Poppy. 'You know what they say, new house new baby!'

Jess thought it was the same for her; not long after she'd moved up from Peckham and Eddie moved in, she discovered she was pregnant. 'So, where's the first meeting gonna be?'

She shot Jess a look over her glasses. 'Well, I'm waiting for someone to volunteer.'

Jess had a feeling this was the real reason behind Ramona's visit but what the hell? She wanted to get to know the other young mums and, if she had them here, she could keep an eye on the tearoom at the same time. 'I don't mind – you can come here if you like.'

'What? You mean in the tearoom?'

'No, here in the conservatory.'

'Brilliant!' Ramona licked her finger to mop up the crumbs. 'Thanks Jess. I'll ring round and let 'em know. Got any more of them scones?'

'I'll give you one to take home if you like?'

'Thanks. Ooh, d'you do takeaway? I reckon you'd make a bomb.'

'D'you know what, you've got me thinking.'

'Yeah, a lot of places do that now, you know, cream teas in pretty boxes and stuff.'

'That's a really good idea. I'll have to look into it.'

There was another tap on the back door. 'Hi Jess, only me!'

'Be back in a tic.' Jess went through to find Janie who had already taken delivery of the clean laundry and was ready to start checking it off. 'Hi Janie, leave that. Come and meet Ramona.'

Janie's heart swelled at the sight of the two women with their children. Yes, her storm magic had worked perfectly.

*

Yesterday had been productive for Laura. After driving out to various towns and villages she had noted two possible shops and had taken their letting details, rung the estate agents this morning and booked some viewings. But the little dilapidated shop in the village was still on her radar. Twice she'd rung Mrs Pemberton-Jones but had been directed to an answerphone on both occasions, so today she was determined to drive up to the hall and see if she could speak to her in person.

The tall iron gates stood open inviting her to drive into the grounds of Leadale Hall, but Laura was surprised at the level of neglect. Surely no one lived here? The grass was a foot high and the carriage drive leading up to the house didn't look as if it'd had any attention for years.

The huge building that loomed up in front of Laura was like something from a horror film. Four wide steps covered in dead leaves led up to a dark porch with two stone pillars. The whole place gave off an air of foreboding. She shivered, parked her white BMW X3 in front of the steps and wondered if a butler would materialise when she rang the ancient bellpull.

There didn't seem to be anyone in. Laura was just about to get back in her car when the heavy black door creaked opened to reveal a scruffy unshaven man in his pyjamas and dressing gown.

'Oh, hello,' said Laura, 'I'm looking for Mr Pemberton-Jones.'

The scruffy man looked her up and down. 'Well, you've found him. Who are you?'

Laura offered her hand, but it was ignored. 'Laura Dean, I'm interested in the empty shop in the village. I believe you're the owner?'

His whiskery eyebrows lifted slightly. 'You want to rent it?'

'Yes, if it suits me.'

'Huh, all right, you'd better come in.' He stood to one side revealing the faded wood panelling and the worn carpet runner. Laura followed him down the hallway with what she assumed were old family portraits on the walls and finally into what looked like the morning room. Miss Havisham came to mind.

He gestured for Laura to take a seat on the cracked and faded Chesterfield while he sat in the armchair by the fireplace. 'I would offer you a cup of something but I'm afraid it's the maid's day off,' said Rudolf, trying in vain to keep up appearances. He self-consciously ran a hand through his unkempt grey hair. 'What sort of business do you intend for the shop?'

'Outdoor clothing for country pursuits, walking shoes and that sort of thing. I've done my research,' Laura said brightly. 'The shop's in a good position for passing trade.'

Huh, thought Rudolf, not the state it was in currently. It would need gutting and he didn't have that sort of money. He glanced at the grandfather clock. Where was Rosemary, goddammit? She was far better at this sort of thing.

Laura couldn't understand his reticence. Judging by the state of the property he needed every penny he could lay his hands on. She tried another tack. 'Does it have any living accommodation?'

He shot her a look. 'There is a flat above, don't know what it's like, haven't ventured in there for donkey's years.'

'Perfect! Can I take a look?'

Where was Rosemary, bloody woman? He didn't have a clue where she'd put the keys. He didn't want to go looking for them but he also didn't want to let this fish off the hook. To have revenue from the shop would be very welcome. Very welcome indeed. 'Look, as far as I'm concerned you can do what you damn well like with it but you really need to speak to my wife.'

'Yes, I have tried a couple of times.' Laura thought he sounded very non-committal, rude even, but the little shop was urging her to speak on its behalf. Maybe if she whetted his appetite? 'I could pay you six months' rent in advance, and I've already arranged a guarantor.'

Pound signs flashed before his eyes. He noticed she wasn't wearing a wedding ring. 'That would be most agreeable, Miss?'

'Dean. Laura Dean. How long would the lease be?'

Good grief. How many more questions? Ten years came to mind but he wasn't sure. It was years since he'd had anything to do with that place. 'I'm not sure. Give me your number and I'll tell my wife to give you a call.'

'Thank you. I'm here until Friday.' She fished in her handbag for a piece of paper and a pen, scribbled her number and handed it to him.

'OK, you can see yourself out.'

Strange man, thought Laura as she found her way to the front door. As she turned to get in her car, she noticed a curtain twitch in one of the upstairs windows.

\*

Mandy was at Top to Toe feeling more out of place than ever. She had loved her time in the Dales and couldn't wait to make it permanent. Since she'd returned, everything about Peckham seemed worn out and tired in comparison.

She only had two clients booked in today and her mind went into overdrive wondering when to ring the estate agents to book viewings for the places they'd seen yesterday. But there was no point in contacting the agents until she knew when Trevor could get time off. Then she had to find out if Jess had any available rooms. She took out her phone and scrolled though the houses again. Her favourite was a barn conversion with a separate annexe, perfect for Carol if she decided to move in with them. The only drawback was that it was too far from the primary school. Mandy knew she would have to cut the cord at some point but not yet – the twins were only eight after all. Another property was a converted chapel, very quirky inside, with plenty of room for them and for Carol but it only had a small garden. Last but not least was a large semi, nicely decorated but it was too similar to theirs. That in itself wasn't a problem, but Mandy really wanted to break the mould and find something with a bigger garden.

She grabbed a coffee from the machine downstairs, avoided Liz in case she asked again when she was leaving, and took it into the staff room. Alone with her thoughts Jess came to mind, working on reception, having a laugh with Sarah and Connie. It all seemed so flat in here now. Their evenings at Saucy Meg's Ale House used to be a riot but that venue had closed down. Everything was telling her to move on.

# TWENTY

Looking forward to her mums and toddlers morning, Jess began tidying up the conservatory, putting some of Eliot's toys away and removing anything that might get knocked over. She set up her iPod dock for the baby songs and went through to the kitchen to organise the refreshments, hoping Janie would be able to handle the tearoom when it got busy.

Eddie looked round from feeding Eliot. 'All right, love?'

She nodded. 'I'll need you in here this morning, though, if you can bear to be parted from your beloved Buick.'

'Why? Where's Kate?'

She shot him a look. 'It's Tuesday, remember? Janie will be here. I can't have the two of them working together and after Saturday night… God, it's a bummer.' Jess dragged a hand through her hair. 'I don't know what to do about that.'

'Well, I don't like the thought of her snooping around and I'm with you on the way she treats Janie.'

'Yeah, and after what Sam told me on Sunday…'

'Look, love, I've told you, we can always get someone to replace her.' Eddie didn't like to see her so downcast. It was happening all too often these days. 'Come here.' He wrapped his arms round her, tilted her chin and brushed her lips with his. She didn't respond. 'Look, I'll stay here and help

Janie if it makes you feel any better. Go and have some happy-clappy time with Eliot and your mates.'

'Thanks, love.'

\*

Mrs Pemberton-Jones had contacted Laura and agreed to meet her outside the shop at 10.30 this morning. Laura had a list of questions to ask her and although both Mrs Pemberton-Jones and her husband seemed a bit evasive, she was hoping they would be amenable when it came to the transaction, *if* the shop matched up to her expectations. She had noticed a public carpark outside the village hall, perfect for her customers, but she hoped there would be a separate parking space or a private garage for her own use. She would have to ask Mrs PJ. Huh! That seemed to be the locals' name for the Pemberton-Jones's, and no wonder – it didn't exactly trip off the tongue. And another reason why Mr PJ had earned his nickname, thought Laura, was probably because he lived in his pyjamas. Gosh! She would love to know what stories lay behind the walls of Leadale Hall.

Laura drew up outside the old shop. She was early. While she waited for Mrs PJ, she explored the space around the side of the property and noticed some double gates. She would've liked to have a look inside, but they were padlocked. Peering over the top she could see a metal fire escape with a tiny balcony.

The sound of footsteps made her turn to see a woman with iron-grey hair wearing a wax jacket and a tweed skirt. She held out her hand. 'Good morning, Rosemary Pemberton-Jones.'

'Yes hello, Laura Dean.'

'Shall we start at the front?'

Laura followed her. 'I was looking to see if there was a parking space or a garage.'

'Yes, there is a space, but it would have to be cleared. Is that your car there?' said Rosemary pointing to the white BMW.

'Yes,' said Laura.

Rosemary lifted her eyebrows. 'I see.' So, it *was* Ms Dean who called at the house the other day. She took out a bunch of keys and proceeded to unlock the faded and peeling dark-blue door. 'I'm afraid you'll have to use your imagination. This place hasn't been trading for years.' She had to push hard before the door finally gave way. Stepping into the shop, she kicked the mountain of post to one side.

The first thing Laura noticed was the musty smell. Once her eyes had adjusted to the gloom she saw three backwash basins on the right-hand side and three long mirrors with shelves on the opposite wall.

'As you can see, it used to be a hair salon,' said Rosemary.

Laura scanned the space while Rosemary clonked towards another door. 'There is a small kitchen at the back,' she said, 'and a loo.'

Laura stood in the centre of the old salon and did a 360. The wallpaper was peeling off and the floor tiles were lifting up in places, but the overall impression was very encouraging.

Rosemary stood watching her. 'What did you say you wanted it for?'

'I want to sell clothing for the great outdoors.'

Rosemary's eyes travelled over Laura. 'I see. Well, you would have to rip out the fixtures and fittings of course. We may be able to come to some arrangement on that, if you really want the shop.'

'Can I see upstairs?'

Rosemary lifted one eyebrow. 'Of course.' She led the way up the staircase accessed from the tiny hallway at the back of the shop.

There was a little kitchen, a bathroom, a double bedroom and a small sitting room. It all needed updating but Laura wasn't afraid of a bit of hard work and, with Marjorie's money, it would be well within her grasp. She felt a prickle of excitement and went to find Mrs PJ who was now looking out of the bedroom window.

'I'm sure, with a bit of work, this would suit me perfectly.'

Rosemary looked round. 'Ah, right, we would have to discuss terms of course. Previously, it was on a short lease, ten years. Would that suit?'

'Ten years sounds perfect.' Laura thought if it was left to the PJs the premises wouldn't be maintained very well, if at all. It would all be down to her anyway. 'Can I suggest an FRI lease?'

Rosemary looked blank.

'All costs of maintenance, repairs and insurance to be met by me?'

Trying not to look too excited, Rosemary pinched her lips together and smoothed the back of her hair. In her experience things like this were too good to be true but this young woman seemed to know what she was about. 'I'll have a word with my solicitor but that sounds quite acceptable. The rent would be due quarterly, in advance. You have a guarantor?'

'Oh yes, already arranged. Could I have a look outside?'

'Of course.'

Laura followed her soon-to-be landlady downstairs to the little kitchen and out to the back yard. Despite being very overgrown with ivy and sapling trees, she could see that, once it was cleared, there would be just enough room for her BMW.

*

Jess had had a fun morning. The kids had played happily together and Eliot had giggled his way through the morning. When the others had gone, Ramona brought the last of the dirty dishes into the kitchen. 'Well, that's the lot. What did you think?'

'Yeah, it was fun.'

'I didn't expect Mark to turn up, though.'

'No, nor did I. He seemed more interested in Eddie's old car but he's good with his kids. He was telling me he's a stay-at-home dad. His wife earns more than he used to, so they switched roles.'

Ramona nodded. 'Makes sense. I can't see my old man doing that, though; I think he's quite relieved when Monday comes round!'

'Are we at yours next week, then?'

'Yeah, but don't expect the same treatment – it'll be a cup of instant and the biscuit barrel!' She strapped Poppy into her buggy.

Jess waved them goodbye and returned to the kitchen to see Janie beaming. She'd managed to keep up with the demand, even when she was left on her own, and everyone was happy. Jess knew it wouldn't have run as smoothly if Kate had been in today!

'I can stay and help with the lunches, if you like?' said Janie.

'Cool,' said Eddie, edging towards the door. 'If you don't need me…'

'Oh right,' said Jess. 'No prizes for guessing where you're off to.'

Eddie shook his head and whispered, 'I'll be in the lounge checking on a few things, OK?'

The penny dropped. 'Oh right.' Jess hoped he wouldn't find any nasty shocks.

## TWENY ONE

After viewing the other shops on her list Laura knew in her heart that the little abandoned shop in Leadale was the one for her. The more she thought about it, the more impatient she was to start planning and designing. This morning, after breakfast, she asked Jess if she could recommend a solicitor. Giles instantly sprang to mind. 'I know a brilliant one as it happens, he's helped me with loads of stuff, but he's in London. Where do you live?'

'At the moment I'm living in Dulwich, South East London.'

Jess's eyes widened. 'Oh my God! That's part of my old stomping ground. Giles's office is in Peckham.'

'Perfect! Do you have his business card?'

'Yeah, I think so. I'll go and check.'

Jess wondered whether to say she knew Giles personally but after giving it some thought she decided against it. She would wait to see if Laura contacted him first. She went to the desk in the lounge and dug out the Morgan Bishop business card, hoping Giles wasn't on one of his sailing jollies. She hadn't heard from him since buying Bracken Farmhouse when he and her sister Shelley had been gallivanting around the French coast on Sea Witch. Shelley had gone back to Australia afterwards and she hadn't heard from her since. But that was Shelley all over.

'Here we are,' said Jess.

Laura read the card. Giles Morgan. Now, why did that name ring a bell?

*

Giles Morgan was indeed in his office, more was the pity. He was still champing at the bit, counting down the days when he could take early retirement and spend some much-needed time on Sea Witch, his beloved forty-foot yacht moored in the Solent. His last proper trip was to La Rochelle with Jess's sister Shelley, two years ago, and he was suffering withdrawal symptoms. Perhaps he could go down at the weekend – the weather looked favourable.

Gloria buzzed his intercom. 'A call for you, Mr Morgan.'

'Can't you deal with it, dammit? What do I pay you for?'

He was met with silence.

Maybe that was a bit harsh. 'Sorry Gloria, put them through.'

After a few seconds a woman's well-bred voice tinkled in his ear. 'Mr Giles Morgan?'

'Speaking.'

'Laura Dean. I was recommended to you by Ms Harvey of Bracken Farmhouse, in Leadale, Yorkshire.'

His frown deepened. Who the hell did he know up there? Then it struck him. Ah, Jessica! Good God. 'Yes, how can I help?'

'I've seen a shop I want to lease in that village but it hasn't been used for years. I'll have to strip the contents. I'm not sure if I need to apply for change of use.'

He was only half listening. He wondered how Jessica's life was shaping up. He hadn't heard from her since she'd opened her business. The fact that she hadn't blown her legacy on meaningless frivolities had totally surprised him. 'I see. Could you email me the details? Change of use, was it?' He doodled on his pad a sketchy yacht.

'Yes, it used to be a hairdressers' and I want to open an outdoor clothing shop.'

'Ah, then you don't need it. Change of use would only apply if you were going to open an eating establishment or something in the financial sector.'

'Oh, good, that's wonderful news.'

'Like I said, if you want me to look into the lease, make sure it's all legal and above board, send me the details and we'll go from there.'

'Thanks.' It sounded to Laura as if he was impatient to get off the phone but she said, 'I'm intending to have it on an FRI lease. '

'Really, do you know what that entails?'

'Yes, I used to work for an estate agent.'

'I see. So, you know you'd need a survey?'

Laura had forgotten all about that but didn't let on. 'Oh, yes, thank you.'

'Just out of interest, who's the landlord?'

Laura didn't really know if it was old PJ or his wife, 'Their name is Pemberton-Jones, they live at Leadale Hall.'

Giles got the picture. Probably some strapped-for-cash landed gentry, and if so, they would bite her hand off for that arrangement. 'Ok, email me the details and I'll be in touch.'

*

Jess and Eddie sat with their heads together going through the accounts on his laptop while Janie held the fort. There didn't seem to be anything amiss.

'Phew,' said Jess, 'what a relief, but I've still got a nasty feeling Kate was up to something.'

Eddie scrolled through the entries once more. 'Well this all looks fine. I can't see anything dodgy. And anyway, why would she be searching through our accounts?'

Jess sighed heavily and rubbed her temples. 'I don't know but I reckon she was interrupted by the power cut. We can't be too careful.'

Eddie pulled her closer, kissed her. 'Like I said, we'll just have to keep this door locked when we're busy or if we go out. Our internet security is watertight so no worries there.'

Jess fell silent. After what Sam had told her she was pretty sure something was going on. Although Kate was a good worker and kept all the rooms in pristine condition, Jess knew that working autonomously gave her the perfect opportunity to have a good snoop around behind her back. Maybe even steal from her. But that was a shocking thought and why would she? As far as Jess knew, Kate and her husband were quite comfortably off in Auntie Ivy's cottage. When Jess took her on, she'd told her that she and Mike were retired and she was only looking for bit of pocket money and something to give her an interest. Jess shuddered. At least she had no worries where Janie was concerned.

*

Laura paid her bill.

'Everything all right for you?' asked Jess.

'Yes, thank you. It's been lovely.'

'Cool. Had any luck with the shop?'

'Yes, thanks, it's all quite exciting but I'll have to come back in a couple of weeks to check on a few things. Can I book a room please?'

Jess checked the bookings on her laptop. 'I'm sorry, when were you thinking? Only all the rooms are taken apart from the single for one weekend in three weeks' time.'

'Oh dear, what about the Dog House?'

Jess looked again. 'Nope, sorry.'

'OK, I'll take that room then please. I'll have to find somewhere more permanent when the builders start work. You don't know of anywhere, do you?'

Jess chewed her lip. 'Nope, sorry, not much about. I've got friends looking for the same thing.'

'I see. Thank you.'

'You're welcome. Have a safe journey.' Jess turned to go then remembered. 'Oh, did you get in touch with Mr Morgan?'

'Oh, yes, thanks for that. It all looks very promising.'

'Awesome. Well, good luck.'

Jess was just about to go upstairs when there was a tap on the back door. It was Ramona.

'Hi Jess. Got some exciting news! You busy?'

Jess stood back while Ramona pushed Poppy in. Jess looked across at Eddie. 'This is Ramona, from toddlers.'

'Oh, hi, how you doing?'

'I'm good thanks.' Ramona turned to Jess, eyes huge behind her glasses, 'You'll never guess...there's a film company coming here and they're looking for extras. You up for it?'

'Oh my God! Am I!'

'Awesome! I've gotta find out a few more details but there's a company called InPictures, they're gonna be using the old church for the auditions, right on our doorstep.'

'Cool, when?'

'Two weeks' time, gives us a chance to get our hair done.'

Jess immediately thought of Mandy who she knew would be up for it. 'How many people are they looking for? '

'I don't think it matters. We just turn up on the day.'

'Fantastic. D'you know what they're filming?'

Ramona shrugged. 'Some period drama, I think, but hey, who cares? It's just something a bit different and it gets us out the house for a few hours.'

Jess wondered about Eliot. She turned to Eddie. 'Would you be up for looking after Eliot for a couple of hours then, love?'

'Sure.' He looked at Ramona, 'You got someone to leave Poppy with?'

'Oops! Good point.'

'No problem, you can leave her here.'

'Oh, cool, thanks Eddie.'

Jess glanced at the kitchen clock. 'Want a coffee?'

'You sure?'

'It's fine. Janie'll be here in a minute and there's always a bit of a lull between breakfast and morning coffee.'

'Well, if you don't mind…'

They took the children through to the conservatory and Eddie was left with his thoughts. His ears had pricked up at the words 'film company'.

# TWENTY TWO

Eddie had seen an available three bed semi to rent ideal for Trevor and Mandy. Hoping to strike before anyone else snapped it up, he'd given it the once-over and told Trevor to come up and have a recce. Luckily Jess had had a cancellation and booked Trevor into the single room for two nights, Ben having agreed to cover for him.

Trevor slammed the car door and arched his back. It had been a slow and tedious journey. He texted Mandy to tell her he'd arrived and entered the kitchen to a hive of activity and delicious aromas.

He gave Jess a hug. 'Mandy sends her love. A shame she couldn't be here.'

'Yeah, I know. Coffee?'

'Please. I didn't stop on the way, just wanted to get here. So, what's new?'

Jess grinned. 'There's a film company staying at the retreat. They're holding auditions. I'm going. I reckon Mandy'll be up for it too.'

Trevor glanced at Eddie. 'You going?'

'Huh, yeah right. I'm looking after the kids and the parlour.' He was itching to give Trevor his news but he bit his tongue. A glance into Jessica's Parlour told him some more customers had arrived looking for a table. He went to serve them. Janie was rushing in and out, clearing tables, preparing drinks.

Jess put a steaming Americano in front of Trevor.

'Eliot asleep?'

Jess looked at the clock. 'Yeah, I need to go wake him – he won't sleep tonight! He's getting to be a right little handful, into everything. He's crawling now and he's started pulling himself up on the furniture.'

Trevor smiled. He could remember when the twins were at that stage. 'That's great. Listen, I'll take this upstairs and go freshen up, OK?'

'Sure. Go get your head down for an hour.'

Trevor put his coffee on the hospitality tray and fell onto the bed. It seemed strange being here without Mandy and the twins and he couldn't remember the last time he'd slept in a single bed but he needed to clinch the rental that Eddie had so kindly told him about. He was also hoping to view three more houses while he was here. The room felt chilly, he jumped up to shut the window and watched the rain falling steadily, soaking the garden. His mind travelled back to when they'd all stayed in the Cow Shed on the warm sunny weekend of the wedding. It seemed months ago. He was tempted to get his head down, as Jess had suggested, but his restless energy wouldn't let him relax. He sipped his coffee and went through the details of the houses again. One in particular stood out from the rest and he hoped it would measure up to expectations when he saw it.

Refreshed, Trevor thanked Eddie again for alerting him to the rental and drove to the next village where the estate agent met him at the door. The house was immaculate, unfurnished and ideally situated for the job with plenty of room for Carol if she wanted to stay. He gave the woman a holding deposit, took some photos and sent them to Mandy. Job done. At least now, if push came to shove, they'd have the ideal place to live while they continued their house-hunting.


Back in Peckham, Mandy showed her mum the pictures of the rental that Trevor had sent.

'Oh, very nice. You'll be able to relax now, then.'

'Yeah, but I'd feel a lot happier if we could find our forever home. It's weird but I feel sort of homeless.'

Carol kept quiet. She felt bereft, even though Mandy, Trevor and the twins hadn't moved yet.

Mandy handed Carol a glass of red and poured another. 'Anyway, what d'you think to this? Jess rang to say they're holding auditions for extras up there in the church retreat; some period drama or something. I really wanna do it.'

Carol smiled. 'I remember when they came here one year, the auditions were held in the old Odeon cinema in the high street.'

'Really? I didn't know about that.'

'It was years ago. When it came to the filming there was an awful lot of sitting around and waiting. I was wishing I'd taken my knitting or a book. I was bored stiff. We had to be there at seven in the morning and didn't get away till eight at night. They did it all on one day, well, the part they needed us for. June and Sue went, too.'

'Did you get fed?'

'Mm, they gave us breakfast but it was a bit of a free-for-all and we didn't get anything else until six. Anyway, you might be luckier but take a snack just in case.'

'OK. What were they filming?'

'I can't remember now. I don't think they even used the scene we were in! But at least we got paid.'

Mandy's eyes widened. 'You got paid?'

'Yes but don't get too excited, it wasn't much. I think it paid for a couple of dresses!'

Mandy shook her head. 'Doesn't matter – it's the experience, right?'

'I suppose so but I wouldn't bother again. You might enjoy it, though.'

*

Before Trevor left to view the houses this morning, Eddie had showed him the Buick in all her glory. Her bodywork had needed a lot of work but, in the end, the paint job had gone like a dream and with the new hood she looked as if she'd just rolled off the production line. Trevor could hardly believe it was the same car. Eddie had proudly lifted the bonnet to reveal a sparkling clean engine to which Trevor had said, 'Blimey Eddie, you could eat your dinner off that!'

Eddie had told Trevor how excited he was that the guy in charge of the auditions had asked him to drive the Buick up to the retreat so he could check it out. 'Yeah, it's a stroke of luck that there's an American guy in the film so fingers crossed the Buick will measure up.'

'Yeah? That's really cool, mate.' Trevor was impressed although he had no leanings in that direction.

All this went through Trevor's mind as he drove through the villages in sunshine. If the houses were disappointing at least he could enjoy his time here.

The first house he'd booked to view was the converted chapel but, although impressive, he couldn't picture them living there. It was a bit cramped and there were too many beams on which to bang his head and very little outside space.

The next one was a large semi but too similar to theirs. That wasn't a bad thing in itself but he knew Mandy wanted a bigger garden. It was also a bit too far out for both his new job and the school. He got back in the car with a heavy sigh. Why was this so difficult? Perhaps they would have to rethink how much they wanted to spend.

He drove on to the next property, a barn conversion, and realised it was in the same village as the rental, well placed for his new job and the primary school. From outside it looked very promising – smart grey window frames, clean lines. As soon as he set foot inside it felt right. Through the bi-fold doors he could see two little girls playing with a black Labrador in the landscaped garden. To the side of the property at the back was a self-contained annexe, all on one level, which would be perfect for Carol, giving him and Mandy their privacy. Perfect!

The couple, Grant and Wendy, invited him to sit in the garden while she made him a cup of coffee. He took his time, breathed in the fresh air and explored the outside space. There were no houses in close proximity, and beyond the garden there were hills as far as he could see. Yeah! This was more like it.

Wendy put the coffee in front of him and sat down. 'We've been using the annexe as a holiday rental. It's all equipped for older people which might be useful.'

'Great. One more question,' said Trevor, 'how soon can you move, only we've sold ours and I'm starting a new job up here next month.'

'No problem,' said Wendy, 'we're going to live with my parents until we can find somewhere.'

Trevor wanted to hug her. 'Brilliant! My wife needs to see it but I'm pretty sure she'll fall in love with it.'

Trevor rang Mandy from the car. 'You really need to see it, love. I've got a feeling this is the one. Look, what if I ring work and tell 'em I'm staying here another day and see if Jess can find room for us?'

'But, that would mean me getting a train and Jess has already said she's fully booked.'

'OK, leave it with me. We can't let this one slip through our fingers.'

*

Kate's inquisitive nose had twitched at the sight of the trailers parked in the paddock next to the church. She hadn't had time to investigate but all had been revealed when she'd heard Jess and her friend Ramona talking about the auditions. It was all working in her favour – she knew Jess and her friends would be out of the house one day next week – but she needed to make sure which day, so this morning she took the opportunity to walk up to the church and do a bit of digging.

The heavy church door creaked open onto a smart reception area. The old pews had been removed leaving a huge cavernous space and down one side it looked like there were separate rooms and a mezzanine floor above. Her heels echoed on the ancient stone, the tomb inscriptions worn away by centuries of footfall. As she walked further in, a door at the back opened and a young guy in jeans and tee shirt swung out. 'Hi, can I help?'

Kate turned on her sweetest smile. 'Er, yes,' she began, her voice echoing, 'am I right in thinking you're holding auditions here, for a film?'

'Yeah, next Wednesday as it happens. I'll get someone to talk to you.' He disappeared and a bald, unshaven man in skinny black jeans took his place. 'Hi there, you were asking about the auditions?'

Kate nodded. 'Is it possible to put my name down? Only I won't be available next week.'

'Yeah, if you like,' he started rummaging around behind the reception desk, found some forms and a pen.

She sidled up to the desk. 'Do you think they'd want me?'

He looked her up and down. 'Maybe. They're looking for older people.'

Kate's face fell. She had half a mind to tell him to forget it but he quickly shoved a form at her. 'You can sit here.' He gestured to the reception desk and left her.

She ticked the appropriate boxes and filled in her details. Oh well, at least the day of the auditions had been confirmed. Her mind skipped ahead to Wednesday when Jess et al would be out of the house. But there was a snag. The day after the storm she had sneaked back to the lounge only to find the door was locked. It had been locked ever since but she would have to try and find a way around that if she was to do a bit more digging. She needed to keep Mrs Morgan happy.

*

Jess had told Trevor she remembered that the lounge sofa pulled out into a double bed. 'Ring Mandy and get her up here. You can't lose that house!'

Although Mandy had been reluctant to get the train, she braced herself for the journey, sat down with her takeaway coffee, ignored the person sitting opposite tapping away on his laptop and tried to relax.

When the train finally pulled into the station her heart leapt at the sight of Trevor waiting for her on the platform.

'Come on,' said Trevor, 'I'll take you straight round to the house. I think it's perfect and think you will too.'

When he pulled up outside the barn conversion Mandy's hand flew to her heart. 'Oh wow, Trev! It's even better in real life.'

Grant and Wendy made themselves scarce while Trevor showed Mandy round the whole house, the open-plan up-to-the-minute kitchen, the airy lounge with the log burner and bi-fold doors onto the garden. She wafted her face. 'Oh Trev...'

He grinned and pulled close. 'Yeah, I know, right. Just think: sunny days... the girls playing in the garden...evenings on the patio with a glass of wine... and that view!'

Mandy couldn't speak for emotion. Finally, she followed him into the self-contained annexe where Mandy was in raptures all over again. 'Oh my God, Trev, I can't believe it. I can see Mum walking around in here, she'll love it.'

'Yeah, job done,' said Trevor. 'Now to tell Jess and Eddie.'

# TWENTY THREE

Laura couldn't bear to be indoors now she was on the brink of a new and exciting life. She'd had a busy morning in town checking out brands of clothing she hoped to sell in her shop and now coffee beckoned.

Carol had only just sat down herself. She glanced at the young woman opposite. How extraordinary! She could swear she was the same person who shared her table last time she was in Café Nero. She surreptitiously watched the woman scrolling on her phone whilst taking dainty bites of her Cherry Bakewell. She seemed totally absorbed. She suddenly beamed at Carol. 'I'm sorry but I simply must tell someone! I'm on the brink of having my own shop and it's all rather exciting.'

'Ooh, how lovely, whereabouts?'

Laura shook her head, the sun catching her chestnut hair. 'Oh, not here, I've found the perfect little property up in the Dales!'

Carol's eyes showed her surprise. 'Well, what a coincidence! My daughter's hoping to move up there very shortly. Her husband's got a transfer. Can I ask where?'

'Leadale.'

'No!'

'Why?'

'That's where my daughter's been staying. Her friend Jess owns the B&B called...'

'...Bracken Farmhouse,' they said in unison.

*

To make sure Buster and Silvester didn't wander off Mandy had put them into their carriers while the removal men cleared the house. With their furniture on its way to the Dales, Mandy and Trevor stood in the centre of the bare lounge and took a minute to reflect.

'End of an era,' said Trevor.

Mandy had a mixture of emotions. She would be sad to say goodbye to their home of ten years, but she knew they were on the threshold of a new and exciting chapter in their lives. 'I'll never forget when we first moved in.'

Trevor drew her into his arms. 'Yeah, and all the refurbishing we had to do!'

'I know but it was fun. So many memories...'

Trevor could see the tears beginning to well up. 'No regrets?'

Mandy bit her lip. 'I'll be sad to say goodbye to it but it is time to move on. I'm looking forward to living in the Dales near Jess and Eddie. I'm sure the twins will love it too, once they get used to their new school and make some friends.'

After dropping the keys off to Chris Jenkins, who wished them well in their new abode, they drove round to the school to pick up the twins who were jumping up and down at the sight of both Mum and Dad at the school gates, but they were a bit put out to see Buster and Silvester locked in their carriers.

'It's only till we get to Grandma's,' said Mandy. 'We can let them roam around the house tonight. But you mustn't let them out in the garden. You hear me? We need to get away early tomorrow. We won't have time to go looking for 'em.'

'Yes, Mum,' they chorused.

In the morning Carol was in tears, as Mandy knew she would be, but she tried to console her. 'Oh, Mum, it won't be long before you can come up and stay. And we'll come down often.'

Carol looked sideways at her. 'No you won't. It's too far to keep travelling up and down. I'll be all right. I've got June and Sue to keep an eye on me.'

'Don't cry, Grandma,' said Keira, and kissed her cheek, which made Carol burst into a fresh bout of sobs.

'We'll see you soon', said Kirsty, and kissed her other cheek.

'Oh, gosh,' said Carol, mopping her eyes, 'go on, all of you! You don't want to get held up in traffic. Have a safe journey and don't forget… I'm only on the end of a phone.'

Mandy bit back her own tears and tried to put on a happy face. She glanced at Trevor – his eyes were moist too. This parting was very different from the one last night at Trevor's parents.' They had congratulated them with a bottle of champagne and waved them off with their blessings.

They all piled into the car, Buster and Silvester secured in carriers on the twins' laps in the back. Buster meowed pitifully for the whole journey but true to form, Silvester slept the whole time.

When they arrived at the rented house the removal van was ready and waiting. Mandy let the cats out in the utility room with their food and water and told the twins to keep that door closed. She'd heard of cats taking years to find their way back to their old house. Kirsty and Keira would be devastated if that happened.

In the evening, when all their furniture was in situ, they all went to Jess and Eddie's where she had a slap-up meal waiting for them. Jess had thought of everything, and had even given them a carrier bag full of food to take home until they could get to a supermarket.

'Oh my God, Jess!' said Mandy, 'I can't believe you've gone to all this trouble.'

'What are friends for?'

'Yeah but…' Feeling suddenly overwhelmed Mandy let the floodgates open. 'Oh God, look at me,' she said, wiping her eyes.

'It's all right, Mum,' said Keira, 'We'll look after you.'

'And Auntie Jess has it all under control,' said Kirsty.

Mandy had to laugh at this. Her girls were growing up. But there was so much to organise that she thought her head would burst. There was also the added problem of finding a car but Eddie had a solution.

'We can take Jess's old Ka out of mothballs!' he turned to her. 'You OK with that, love?'

'Yeah, course. I don't use it much now.'

'It'll do you until you find something else,' said Eddie.

Mandy looked at Jess. 'Well, if you're sure, only I know how much you loved that car.'

Jess smiled as she remembered driving her bubble-gum pink Ka around Peckham and the day when Giles literally fell into her life. One Monday morning she'd been sitting in a traffic queue and a man had stumbled in front of her car and twisted his foot trying to cross the road. She had run him to work at Morgan Bishop, the solicitors', and he had given her his business card; Giles Morgan. Thinking all her dreams had come true, she'd rung the number on the business card and Giles had asked her to lunch. The second date was at his yacht club, but she still cringed at the thought of Lydia barging in and embarrassing her. Jess and Shelley had two nicknames for her: The Bitch from Hell and Cruella.

But it slowly dawned on Jess that it was Eddie she loved. He had always been there for her hoping that one day Jess would fall back in love with him. Giles had come in very useful when it came to the will, though. But she would never forget that day in his office when The Bitch from Hell had burst in claiming the legacy belonged to her. Giles and his father had soon sent her packing.

And now Jess had everything she wanted: a loving partner, her beautiful little boy and a thriving business. 'Yeah, the Pink Peril should get you around until you find something else.'

'Thanks Jess,' said Mandy, 'that's a great help.'

Eddie knew what Jess had been thinking. He winked at her. Maybe now was the time. He got down on one knee, dug deep into his pocket and held up a tiny box. 'Jess, I know it's been a long time coming, but...' he opened the box to reveal a sparkling engagement ring, 'will you marry me?'

'Oh my God! Will I.' She flung her arms round him.

'Here,' said Eddie, slipping the diamond cluster on her finger, 'I hope it fits.'

Jess's eyes shone. 'Oh my God, it's gorgeous, Eddie.'

'And so are you!'

Mandy's heart filled. She jumped up and flung her arms round them both. 'I'm so happy for you. This is the perfect end to a perfect day.'

Trevor patted Eddie on the back. 'Yeah, congratulations, mate.'

Kirsty turned up her nose. 'Does that mean we have to be bridesmaids again?'

They all laughed through their happy tears.

\*

Laura parked in Priory Square and checked her appearance in the rear view-mirror. She had emailed a copy of the shop lease to Giles Morgan and now she needed him to witness her signature. She certainly didn't want Roger's name on the contract, her mother was away and time was running out to find anyone else.

She pushed open the engraved glass door to Morgan Bishop and stepped up to the reception desk.

A thin mousy-looking woman looked up from her screen. 'Can I help you?'

'Yes, I have an appointment with Mr Morgan.'

'Can I have your name?'

'Laura Dean.'

The woman checked her screen and buzzed through to his office. 'Ms Dean to see you, Mr Morgan.'

Laura heard his response. 'Show her in would you, Gloria.'

Giles Morgan. Laura wondered again where she'd heard that name before. It was somewhere in her distant memory, but it wouldn't surface.

He was standing in his favourite spot staring out the window. He turned when she entered. 'Ah, take a seat.'

He was younger than his voice implied but she still couldn't place him. She glanced around briefly before sitting in the chair in front of his desk. His office was exactly how she'd imagined it; stuffy and old-fashioned but elegant.

'You have the required documents?' He took them from her without looking up. 'Thanks.'

She watched him going through her passport and driving license, head down, concentrating.

He looked up to see her staring at him. He averted his eyes, cleared his throat. 'I'll just get these photocopied,' and strode out of the room.

Yes, now she remembered! Boarding school! Good God. He was always a quiet boy, a loner, didn't have many friends. In fact, she couldn't remember him having *any* friends. But she'd had a massive crush on him back then. It came as no surprise that he'd gone into the family business. He'd always been a studious boy quietly getting on with his lessons. Ha! How funny that she should bump into him again all these years later.

Giles came back with the documents. 'Can I help you with anything else?'

'Yes, I would like you to witness my signature on the contract,' said Laura, placing it in front of him.

'Oh yes, of course.' He picked up his pen and wrote with a flourish.

She remembered that too.

Giles glanced up at her. 'You're renting a shop in the Dales but you live in Dulwich?'

Laura nodded.

'Forgive me, I don't mean to pry but…'

'…I'm separating from my husband and I need my own income. I plan to live above the shop.'

'I see. I believe you've been staying up there. What's the name again?'

'Bracken Farmhouse, it's a delightful place.'

'And the owner?'

'Jess Harvey. She runs it with her partner, Eddie.'

Yes! It *was* Jessica's establishment. Curiosity was tugging at him. 'Is she busy?'

'Yes, very. And she's got a toddler. I don't know how she manages.'

Giles thought about this. He couldn't picture Jessica with a child.

'I tried to book again, so that I could stay up there and keep an eye on the building work, but she's fully booked right through the summer.'

His eyes ran over Laura's face, her hair. 'I'm sorry, but...do I know you from somewhere?'

She smiled and looked into his deep brown eyes. Let him stew for a bit longer. She was enjoying this. 'It was a long time ago.'

Giles frowned, shook his head. 'No, I'm sorry you'll have to enlighten me.'

Laura lifted her eyebrows. 'Boarding school?'

'Good God! That *was* a long time ago.' He had a vague memory of Laura waiting around in the quadrangle for a chance to speak to him, but he was always too shy. He glanced at his watch. He longed to get out of the office and saw his chance. 'Look, I don't want to sound pushy, and say no if you'd rather not, but we can continue this conversation over lunch, if you'd like?'

\*

Eddie hadn't been able to sleep for excitement. Today was his big day; he was going to drive his pride and joy up to the retreat to show her off to Guy Lockhart from the film company. Yesterday Jess had been gobsmacked at the car's transformation – gleaming burgundy paintwork, sparkling white hood and whitewall tyres. Now he couldn't wait to show her off to the one person who could be his ticket into the film industry, although he did have a couple of niggling doubts: What if she wasn't right for the film they were shooting? What if they didn't want an American car? He had that covered if that was the case; he'd taken delivery of a black Wolseley 6/90 a few days ago. He'd done his research and found out that the police had used that model in the 50s. He had everything crossed hoping they might even want both cars.

Eddie pulled into the grounds of the retreat and a guy standing on the step instantly stubbed out his cigarette and came to peer at the burgundy Buick. It gleamed in the sun.

'Hi, I'm Guy. So, this is it?'

'Yeah, what d'ya think?' Eddie got out and left the door open to show off the interior.

Guy walked all around the car, stroked his chin. 'She's a beaute and no mistake.'

Eddie felt his heart swell with pride. 'Get in, if you like?'

Guy sat in the cream leather seat and ran his hands round the steering wheel. Eddie let out the breath he'd been holding but Guy gave nothing away. He went to the church door and called out, 'Tristan? Come and have a look at this.'

Another, older man sauntered over to take a look.

'What d'ya think?' said Guy.

'Yeah, could be ideal for Walt.' Tristan walked all around the car, ran his hands over the bonnet. 'How does she handle?'

'Like a dream,' said Eddie. 'Get in and I'll show you.'

Tristan pinched his top lip. 'Can you put the hood down?'

Eddie released the catches but the hood got stuck halfway making a crunching sound. His stomach turned over. Guy and Tristan stared at him. 'I'll sort it,' he said, breaking out in a sweat. 'It's only something minor.'

'OK. What else you got to show us?'

Eddie's heart was pounding. 'I've got a Wolseley 6/90 – I can have it ready in a few days.'

Tristan nodded. 'Cool. Anything else?'

'Not at the moment,' said Eddie, crossing his fingers behind his back and hoping Mr Fairview would come up with the goods yet again. 'What you looking for?'

'Well, anything British really. Austin, Morrris…' He shrugged. 'As long as it's a good fit. It needs to be no later than 1952.'

'OK. I'll get onto it, but what about the Buick? You interested?'

'Yeah, yeah, as long you get that hood fixed. Come into the office and we'll go through a few details for insurance purposes.'

Eddie unlocked his fingers and followed them.

*

Kate was fuming – she'd had a text from InPicures – she was not suitable, but this wasn't the only thing that was bugging her. Not only had Eddie and Jess started locking the lounge door but her hours had been cut and another woman had been drafted in to help with the changeovers. On top of that Kate had a horrible feeling that Mrs Morgan was back in the UK and an even nastier feeling that she might pay Bracken Farmhouse a visit. She braced herself for her weekly phone call, pressed her keypad and hoped for the best.

'Lydia Morgan.'

'Yes, hello, it's me, Katherine.'

'Ah, Katherine, so nice of you to check in,' she said, sarcastically.

Kate's pulse went up a notch. 'I'm sorry…I haven't had a chance…'

'Not good enough! If you're not up to the task I'll find someone who is.'

'But…I'm working on it.' She didn't want to tell Mrs Morgan that they had probably rumbled her.

'What about the painting?'

Kate took a deep breath. 'Ah, yes, er…I've got an idea for that…'

'Really.'

'Yes. What if I suggest that they need to get it professionally cleaned?'

'And?'

'Well, I could ask Eddie to help me put it in my car…'

'Ha, don't make me laugh. No, I have a much better idea. I know a restorer who can come and take a look. He'll convince the Blonde Tart that she needs to have it cleaned to increase its value by a few thousand – I'm sure she won't be able to turn that down! And he'll take it away for you. All you need to do is give her my restorer's name. Can I trust you with this?'

'Yes, of course.'

'Good. I'll be in touch.'

# TWENTY FOUR

Janie was hoping the guy who had been coming in lately would pay the tearoom another visit today. She had noticed he came at roughly the same time, sat in the same spot and asked for the same fruit scone and coffee every time. So predictable was he that she could almost have it ready for when he arrived. He was a man of few words, but he seemed gentle and he had the kind of smile that made Janie's skin tingle. She could tell he liked her.

'All right there, Janie?' asked Eddie, cleaning down one of the worktops. 'You're looking pleased with yourself.'

Her face lit up. 'Am I?'

'Spill, or are you keeping it to yourself?'

'I don't know what you mean.' She was enjoying this. She was very rarely the focus of anyone's attention.

'Anyway, nice to see you happy. Job shaping up all right?'

'Aye, with a bit of luck I'll soon be able to pay off me rent arears!'

Eddie winked. 'Cool.'

Armed with her pad and pen Janie went through to the tearoom. She looked at the clock. No, it wasn't his time yet, but there were two women sitting at table three. They stopped talking as she approached.

'A pot of tea for two and two pieces of your wonderful chocolate sponge, please.'

'Certainly,' Janie wrote it down. 'Will that be all?'

'Yes, thank you.'

Janie had done the Tarot last night and hoped she'd interpreted the cards correctly. Preparing a tray and filling a teapot she heard footsteps and a chair dragging on the floor. *Keep calm and try to act normal.* She clattered on the lid and set it on a tray with the cups and saucers, napkins and cutlery. He was there! She could sense him. Trying not to look, she went into the tearoom and lifted the lid on the chocolate sponge, her hand shaking. Tingling with anticipation and without looking up, she took the cake back to the kitchen, completed the tray and served the two ladies who expectantly removed their elbows from the table.

'Mm, that looks delicious,' said one.

'It is, I've had it before,' said the other.

She saw him from the corner of her eye, took out her pad and pen and tried not to get flustered.

'Hello.' His velvet voice made her knees go weak.

She pre-empted him. 'An Americano with skimmed milk and a fruit scone and butter?'

'Please.' His broad smile mirrored hers.

She wanted to shout from the rooftops! He's here! And he's come to see *me*! She was all of a dither, could hardly keep the coffee in the cup as she placed it on the tray.

Thankfully Eddie had just taken some fruit scones out of the Aga so she didn't have to go back into the tearoom for one. She arranged his tray and took it in, set in front of him.

'Thanks, lovely as always.'

'Ta, I'll pass it on.' She could feel him watching her every move. Dare she ask if he was local? Where he lived? No, the words died on her tongue. She skipped into the kitchen and looked for something with which to keep busy and saw Eddie emptying the dishwasher. 'I'll do that.'

'If you like. You OK if I nip over the workshop?'

'Sure.'

'Jess'll be down in a minute. She's getting Eliot ready to go to Ramona's.'

Janie began putting the crockery away when she heard some more activity in the tearoom. Where had all those people come? Two full tables inside and, through the doorway, she could see another table of four outside. She left the dishwasher and hurried through to take their orders. She must try to look super-efficient, no slip-ups. She wanted to give him a good impression.

Jess called out. 'You OK Janie?'

'Excuse me,' Janie said to a customer, 'I'll be back in a bit.' Jess was putting Eliot in his buggy. 'It's really busy but I think I can handle it. Eddie's nipped over the workshop.'

Jess glanced through to the tearoom, two more people had come in. 'I'll go get him.'

Janie went back to serve, all the while sensing those eyes on her. She knew he would be ready to pay his bill any minute and she didn't want Eddie to take his money.

She was preparing another tray when she noticed he was there standing by the till.

'I'll get that,' said Eddie, but Janie got there before him.

She took a deep breath. 'Everything all right for you?'

His warm brown eyes seemed to sink into her soul. 'Mm, more than all right.'

Janie felt her face flush and her stomach flip. She put the money in the till and gave him his change and was about to serve another customer when he steered her to one side and lowered his voice.

'Hey, I was wondering…'

Her heart was pounding. 'Yes?'

'I don't know how you feel about this, but, er,' he took a breath, 'how would you like to go for a drink one evening?'

'Oh, I'd love to!'

Eddie, who was dishing up two slices of Bakewell tart, listened as they made their arrangements. He was pleased for her. It was about time she had some luck.

Janie watched her customer walk down the drive and turned to see Eddie's beaming smile. 'Don't say a word!'

'Wouldn't dream of it!'

\*

Jess, Mandy and Ramona all thought they stood a pretty good chance of getting accepted for the film extras. Jess a typical English blonde, Mandy with her burgundy hair, and Ramona a brunette, they made a pleasing threesome. Eddie had said they all looked awesome and wished them luck. Janie was taking charge of the tearoom, much to Jess's surprise and delight, and Eddie was looking after the kids. It was mayhem with Kirsty and Keira, Poppy and Eliot all in the conservatory. Jess had shut the door on the noise, thankful for a morning off, and all three women had set off for the retreat.

As they walked, Jess told them about the Buick being accepted for the film and how excited she was for Eddie. 'Yeah, he's chuffed to bits. He's got another old car that he's doing up, a black one, they might use that as well.'

'That's awesome, Jess,' said Mandy.

'Yeah,' said Ramona, 'wicked!'

When they arrived at the retreat there didn't seem to be anyone around, no parked cars.

'Seems odd, don't you think?' said Mandy.

'It does a bit. Anyway, let's go in and see,' said Jess.

They entered to find a few people milling around and a guy sitting at reception. 'You here for the auditions?'

They all nodded.

'OK, take a form and a pen.' He pointed to a stack on the desk. 'When you're done, they'll want your measurements.' He indicated a table further down the nave where a woman was dishing out tape measures.

Mandy and Jess looked at each other. Jess shrugged.

'Come on,' said Ramona, 'let's make a start. There's a table over there we can use.'

'I thought it'd be rammed,' said Jess, scanning the place.

'Maybe it's cause we're early.' Mandy was busily filling in all the details on the form. At the top was written The Manor House Murders. 'Hang on – shall I put the address of the rented house or the barn?'

Jess was still watching the other people and waiting to see if anyone else arrived. 'I'd put both.'

'Good point,' said Mandy, 'I'll put a note as well.' She scribbled away. 'That's it. I'm done.'

'Me too,' said Ramona, throwing her pen down on the table. 'I'll go and queue up for a tape measure.'

Filling in her form, Jess said to Mandy, 'I don't know what I was expecting but it wasn't this!'

'No, I know what you mean.' Mandy turned to scan the rest of the retreat. There didn't seem to be anything happening apart from the woman photographer who had set up an area to take the applicants' portraits.

Ramona took a tape, found an alcove with a shelf and began measuring her bust, her waist but when she looked at her hip measurement, her eyes popped. She hadn't realised she'd got so much bigger since having Poppy. She really must cut down on the biscuits.

Jess and Mandy were measuring each other and comparing notes when Ramona asked them to help measure her height, but she turned her form over before they could see her dress size. Next, they queued up to have their photos taken and watched one guy stand in front of the plain blue background posing for the camera. He'd obviously gone to a lot of trouble to look like a fifties film star with his dark hair greased back, and thought he looked the part. He smoothed his hair and flashed his toothpaste smile. 'How d'you want me?'

The woman shook her head and sighed impatiently. 'For heaven's sake, just stand normally, arms by your side.'

Jess pinched her lips together and avoided eye contact with Mandy in case she set her off giggling. That guy sauntered off and another swaggered up to take his place. Then it was Mandy's turn. She stepped up to the background and tried to keep a straight face and stared straight at the camera.

'Good God,' said the photographer, 'don't look so serious. Looks like you're wanted for murder.'

'Quite fitting, then!'

This set Jess and Ramona snorting with laughter. Mandy rearranged her face and the camera clicked. Then it was Jess's turn, but she caught Mandy's eye and starting giggling all over again.

The photographer, hands on hips, waited for Jess to compose herself. 'Honestly, like a load of kids. When you're ready, I haven't got all day.'

Jess was about to come up with a witty remark, but instead, she moistened her lips, stood tall and looked straight at the camera.

'OK,' said the woman, 'Next.'

Feeling self-conscious about her weight, Ramona stepped up the background and breathed in.

'Is that the best you can do?' asked the woman. 'Don't look so stiff. It's not a mug shot.'

Ramona took a second and tried to relax.

'OK,' said the woman, disinterested. 'Hand your forms in at the desk.'

'Is that it?' asked Jess.

'Unless you can think of anything else?'

Mandy and Ramona looked at each other, then at Jess.

'Well, what happens next?' asked Jess. 'When will we know?'

'If you're selected they'll text you sometime in the next few days. You've put your mobile numbers on the forms? Good, you might be called for a crowd scene, a garden party or something like that. We're not sure at the moment.'

'OK, cool, and that's at Thornwood Manor?'

The woman nodded. 'At the moment,' and turned back to take the next photo.

Back in the conservatory, Jess was greeted with the happy sound of Eliot chuckling – Kirsty was holding his hands and walking him slowly up and down while Eddie watched. Keira was playing with Poppy and Janie was in and out of the kitchen. Everything seemed to be running like clockwork.

'We'd better go,' said Mandy. She called to the twins, 'Come on, let's be having you.'

'Aw,' said Kirsty, 'do we have to?'

'Yes, we do, come on.' Mandy turned to Jess. 'I'll catch you later.'

'Yeah, me too,' said Ramona and began strapping a protesting Poppy into her buggy.

When they'd gone Eddie dragged a hand through his hair. 'Phew, I don't know what's worse – looking after the kids or the tearoom! How'd it go?'

'I dunno, it was a bit weird,' said Jess. 'We just had to fill in some forms and have our photos taken.'

'Is that all? Didn't they ask you to do anything?'

Jess shook her head. 'They just told us we'll get a text.'

'Oh well, you never know.'

Eliot's chuckles made Jess and Eddie turn to see him take a few steps unaided then he flopped onto his bottom.

'Oh wow!' said Jess, picking him up and smothering him in kisses. 'You clever boy!'

'Fantastic,' said Eddie, 'and we were both here to see it!'

\*

Kate was not happy. She was hoping to have a sly poke around while Jess and her friends were up at the retreat, but the lounge door was still locked. And that daft cow Janie was taking her place in the tearoom otherwise she might've been able to get into Jess's laptop. Damn. She would have to have another rethink.

# TWENTY FIVE

Trevor came home to find Mandy and the girls in the garden. He slung his car keys on the sideboard and rubbed the back of his neck. He had thought the new job was what he wanted but there were still the same problems, albeit on a smaller scale. Should he look for something else, something totally different? But retail was all he'd known since he'd left school. He thought of Eddie and Jess – they'd taken a different turn and now had a thriving business. Well two, if you counted Eddie's classic cars.

Mandy shot through the door and gave him a big hug and he felt the day's tension begin to drain away. Perhaps he was being too hasty. She poured him a large glass of Merlot. 'Let's sit in the garden. It's too nice to be indoors.'

They sat on the bench overlooking the rolling hills. This is what they had moved for, thought Trevor, a better life away from the hustle and bustle of London, but his job as supermarket manager didn't fit the pattern.

'What's wrong?' asked Mandy, ever intuitive.

Trevor shook his head. 'Oh, nothing much, just the usual stuff to do with work.'

'Not what you expected?'

Trevor screwed up his nose. 'Early days, we'll see. What you been up to?'

'Apart from the auditions,' she gestured inverted commas, 'when we went back to Jess's Kirsty was walking

Eliot up and down in the conservatory. He was giggling away, bless him. Jess rang me a little while ago to say he'd taken his first steps, on his own! He just got up, tottered a few steps and fell back on his bum.'

Trevor brightened. 'That's fantastic!'

'Yeah, except she'll have her work cut out now. He'll be into everything. I don't know how she does it. She looks knackered.'

Trevor nodded. 'But Eddie does his fair share. And there's Janie.'

Mandy slid her eyes sideways. 'Eddie's mostly in the workshop messing about with those old crocks and Janie can't work with Kate. Something about her I don't like.'

'Who, Kate?'

Mandy nodded. 'Yeah, I dunno but she's always poking her nose in. I wouldn't trust her as far as I could spit.'

Trevor smiled; his wife was rarely wrong about people.

'I might ask Jess what she thinks to me helping out. She could do with another pair of hands.'

'But you've never done stuff like that.'

'No but how hard can it be? It's still dealing with customers and I'm used to that.'

Trevor nodded. 'True. Anyway, I'm starving.' He glanced at his watch. 'Fancy going to the Green Man?'

Mandy's eyes lit up. 'Do I!' she kissed him. 'And maybe you'll get your fish pie this time.' She shouted to Kirsty and Keira. 'Come on you two, we're going out for dinner.'

'Yess!' Kirsty punched the air.

'Are we going to Auntie Jess's?' asked Keira.

'Not this time,' said Trevor, 'we're going out, out.'

*

Janie was all of a dither, excited but anxious. She'd changed her dress three times and she still didn't know whether to wear her hair up or down. She was out of practice. She didn't want to overdo it, but she did want to look as if she took a pride in her appearance. Darren, she knew his name now, was calling for her at 8pm. She had another fifteen minutes. Thinking that he might come back to her house later, she quickly hid her *Prediction* and *Kindred Spirit* magazines under the armchair cushion. She wondered what he'd think to her spiritual beliefs. She would wait until she got to know him better, *if* she got to know him better, before she sprang those on him. They were only going for a drink, she told herself. But deep down she longed for it to be more, to find that he was everything she wanted in a partner.

Trevor pulled into the carpark behind the Green Man. It was a warm evening and Mandy, whose eyes were everywhere as she walked through the gate, suggested they sit in the garden.

'It's a Zen garden!' she exclaimed.

'What's a Zen garden?' asked Trevor.

'Well, I think it comes from the Japanese, originally meant for meditation, Buddhism and stuff like that.'

While Trevor went to sit at a table with Kirsty and Keira, Mandy took a moment to study the rock garden all along one side. A small Buddha statue sat centre stage while bonsai trees and moss surrounded the gently rippling water feature, all set within white gravel raked in circles. 'We could do something like that in our garden, Trev. It's very calming.'

'Cool,' said Trevor, 'but I like to see a few flowers.' He picked up a menu. His face fell. 'They haven't got fish pie on tonight.'

'It's probably on the specials board,' said Mandy. 'Go and see.' She turned to Kirsty and Keira eying up the white gravel. 'Now you two – don't go getting any ideas – it's not a playground, all right?'

Mandy gave them each a menu and pointed to the children's section. She suddenly thought of her mum and wondered what, or if, she would be eating tonight. Mandy had a sneaky feeling she didn't eat properly. Whenever Carol had the twins to stay she would only feed them, saying she'd had something earlier. She needed to get her up here soon, give her a boost.

Trevor came back with a big smile on his face.

'Oh, so that's you sorted, then,' said Mandy, and went inside to check the specials board herself.

As Janie and Darren walked to the Green Man, he told her about the retreat in the village where he was staying. 'It's for people who want to take some time out from their busy lives, to meditate and perhaps for some spiritual healing, or just to enjoy the surroundings. There's a room for quiet prayer and four cells with shared facilities on the ground floor...'

'...Cells?' cut in Janie, 'sounds more like prison!'

'Not at all, it's what they call the individual rooms in a monastery.'

'Oh? I never knew that.'

'Yes, the whole place is very tranquil, apart from yesterday when they were holding auditions for a film. That didn't bother me, though.'

'Yes,' said Janie, 'Jess and her friends went.'

'Not you?'

'No, not my scene. I was looking after the tearoom, 'she said proudly.

They entered the pub to the sound of tinkling glasses and convivial chatter. Darren stepped up to the bar. 'What'll it be?'

Janie, who only drank when she could afford it, had to think. She'd never been one for spirits of the liquid kind and couldn't remember the last time she'd set foot in the pub. She decided on Jess's favourite. 'I'll have a glass of pinot grigio, please.'

'Inside or out?'

Janie looked around the noisy bar and suddenly felt overwhelmed. 'Outside, I think.'

'OK, go and find us a table.'

*Us,* she liked the sound of that. The last time Janie had ventured into the Green Man she was sure it hadn't looked like this. The guy with dreadlocks behind the bar looked interesting too. How had she not noticed before? She ducked under the low doorway and up a step and into the garden. This was right up her street. She'd had no idea there was a Zen garden here – it was completely hidden from the road. Ignoring the other customers, she sat at a table near the water feature. It soothed her. She had books on Buddhism and other world religions, found them all fascinating, and she wondered again if Darren would find her too wacky. Her heart swelled at the sight of him walking towards her with the drinks. He sat down and passed her the glass of chilled white wine. 'Cheers! Some place.'

Janie nodded. 'Aye.' She took a sip of the Pinot Grigio. It tickled her taste buds and calmed her. She wondered why she was so nervous.

Darren sipped his ale and licked his lips. 'Mm, so, tell me a little about yourself.'

That's why. Oh God, where to start. She didn't want to give him the same sob story she'd given Jess. She decided on the safe option. 'Well, I live on me own, I've got a cat called Gandalf and two rescue donkeys, Neptune and Pluto.'

Darren laughed. 'I like it. Sorry, carry on.'

'That's it really. There's not much more to tell. You know where I work and until a couple of months ago, I didn't even have that.' Oh dear, that came out wrong.

Darren studied her face. She felt she could drown in those eyes. 'Any family?' he asked.

Janie shook her head. 'I won't bore you with all that.' She took another sip of wine and tried to change the subject. 'What do you do? For work, I mean?'

He smiled, taking his time, and Janie wondered what he was going to tell her.

'I'm a history teacher at the sixth form in Skipton. I enjoy it but it all gets a bit much after a while – never-ending paperwork, getting pupils through their exams. That's why I like the retreat.'

A history teacher, crikey! She hoped he didn't think her dense. She searched for something else to ask him and fell upon another safe option. 'Do have any family?'

'None of my own, sadly, but my sister has three boys. They live in York. My parents live up in the Orkneys but I manage to get up there twice a year.'

'I've never been there.'

'No? It's very beautiful but very remote. Miles of open space and the beaches are to die for. They moved up there when my dad retired.' He saw her glance at his left hand. 'Don't worry, I'm not married!' He drained his glass. 'Want another?'

'I'll get these,' said Janie.

'No, you won't, I wouldn't dream of it.'

Janie watched him go then her gaze fell on the family eating a meal two tables away. Mandy and Trevor and their twins! Without the protection of the tearoom she suddenly felt exposed. She looked away.

Mandy whispered to Trevor. 'Don't look now, but isn't that Janie?'

'Yes, it is!' shouted Kirsty, grinning and waving at her.

'Oh God, be quiet and eat your dinner,' said Mandy.

'I have, I don't want any more.'

'Well just sit there and wait till we've finished ours. Janie doesn't want to be bothered with you.'

'Is she on a date night?' asked Keira.

Trevor grinned at Mandy. 'What are they like?'

'I dunno but I feel for the poor woman.'


After their meal, Trevor and Mandy decided to pop in on Jess and Eddie. He called out from the workshop, 'Door's open, Jess is in the lounge.'

Mandy ventured in to find Jess sprawled out on the sofa. 'I thought we'd just pop in as we were in the Green Man, but say if not. You look knackered.'

Jess jumped up, yawned and headed to the kitchen. 'Drink?'

'We're good, thanks,' said Trevor.

Eddie poked his head round the door. 'Everything all right?'

Mandy nodded. 'We've just been in the Green Man for a meal...'

'...It was really nice,' butted in Kirsty.

'Yeah, and guess what?' said Mandy. 'We saw Janie... with a man!'

Jess was instantly awake. 'Oh my God! Spill!'

'You staying for a drink?' said Eddie.

Mandy looked at Trevor who looked at the twins and then at his watch. 'OK, just for a while.'

Eddie went to the fridge for two beers, handed one to Trevor. 'How's the job?'

Trevor's expression spoke volumes.

'Like that is it?'

Trevor glanced at Mandy who had her worried face on. 'Still, early days and all that.'

Jess took Mandy into the lounge. 'Come on, I wanna hear all about Janie!'

The twins followed them and left Eddie and Trevor in the kitchen.

'So wassup, mate,' said Eddie. 'I thought you had this lark all sorted.'

Trevor blew out his cheeks, 'So did I. But all I've done is exchange one big problem for smaller one.' He took a mouthful of his beer. 'I shouldn't be drinking this. I've gotta drive home.' He pushed it to one side.

Eddie's thoughts went back to when all this started. 'Have you told Mandy?'

Trevor shook his head. 'She thinks it's just a few teething troubles.'

'Look, I haven't said anything to Jess but, if you really can't hack it, I might have a job for you.'

Trevor's eyes had grown to twice their normal size. 'Doing what?'

'Property manager!'

'What? This place? But I don't know the first thing about hospitality.'

'That's OK, I can tell you how to run it, but I could do with you to look after the accounts. I'm letting things slide and Jess is so tired all the time. We don't get a minute. Eliot's getting older and it was only by chance that we saw him take his first steps yesterday.'

Trevor nodded. 'OK, I'll think on it. Cheers Eddie.'

# TWENTY SIX

Laura pushed open the door on the old hairdresser's and stood in the dark musty-smelling space. At least the structural survey hadn't given her any nasty shocks. The builders had started work and the fixtures and fittings had now been stripped out, but she'd decided to keep the three full-length mirrors for the changing rooms. The next stage was going to entail new units and plumbing in the little downstairs kitchen, the loo and, later on, the flat upstairs. The last thing on her list was to employ a shop fitter and a decorator before ordering the stock. She envisaged 'Rain or Shine' above the shop window, the doorbell tinkling and satisfied customers.

She reacquainted herself with the rooms upstairs. The day was very warm, the flat felt stuffy and airless so she opened the landing window. There was a lot of work to do to transform the flat into the one in her mind's eye, but she was pleased that the kitchen door led out to a fire escape. Yes, she could transform it with a few pots of flowers to brighten it up. She imagined sitting with a glass of wine and a book and, if the trees were trimmed, she might even have a view.

Laura was itching to strip off the 70s sunflower wallpaper in the sitting room and the overpowering pink bedroom paper but at least both rooms had sound floor boards that she intended to sand. All this was going to cost thousands. Luckily her mother had given her a substantial sum but she would have to eke it out. And all this for a building that wasn't even hers! But, maybe in the future, if her business became the success she hoped for, she could make the PJs an offer?

She locked the kitchen door and ran downstairs, took out her phone to make some notes and noticed a message from Giles. A smile spread across her face.

'*Have fun with the shop. If I can help you with anything else don't hesitate to get in touch.*'

Her phone alerted her to another text that wiped the smile off her face. Roger, '*We can't go on like this. I'm going to see my solicitor about a divorce. I suggest you do the same.*'

\*

Eddie had erected the parasols in the tea garden this morning before starting work on the Wolesley. Today was going to be another scorcher; the workshop was already airless even with the doors open. But he was pleased with the bodywork on this one. It gleamed like jet and only needed the minimum of work to bring it up to scratch. And Mr Fairview had come up trumps yet again – an Austin 10 which was under wraps, awaiting Eddie's attention.

InPictures had confirmed they wanted all three cars! He couldn't believe his luck. Guy and Tristan were very happy with what he had shown them so far, and he'd managed to sort out the hood on the Buick. That had been a tricky moment – he didn't want anything like that to happen again. He was encouraged by the amount of money they were paying him too; it would mean his business taking off big time.

In fact, things were looking up all round. Trevor had handed in his notice at the supermarket and was looking forward to starting his new job as property manager and Mandy had started working in the tearoom. She was enjoying it and Eddie couldn't believe the change in Janie. Everything was working out perfectly all except for one nasty little bug in the ointment. He hoped Kate would soon be history but that was Jess's department.

Jessica's Parlour was rammed, customers in shorts and tee shirts milling around waiting for tables. Jess had had to bake more scones and replenish the coleslaw and salads while Janie and Mandy were rushing in and out, serving and taking money.

Outside people were enjoying the warm sunny day, dogs panting beneath the tables. Mandy had refilled their water bowls twice. She took her tray back to the kitchen and wiped her forehead. 'Phew, Jess. I'm melting.'

'Yeah, me too. Keep your water topped up.'

Janie checked on the kids in the conservatory. It was boiling hot in there, so she told Kirsty and Keira to go into the garden and play. It was cooler out there under the trees. But Jess wanted to keep Eliot where she could see him, in the kitchen. He was happily playing on the floor with his toys in the space outside the utility room.

Janie took some cold drinks out to the twins and as she made her way back to the kitchen, she spotted Darren at the door. She felt all tingly. 'Hi.'

His sultry gaze travelled over her. 'You know I'm leaving tomorrow?'

She nodded. 'Aye. I wish you weren't.'

'Me too but my parents are expecting me. Can I see you tonight, though?'

'Of course.' She reached up to kiss him just as Kate barged past with the laundry bundle and knocked her flying.

Darren shot her daggers. 'Hey, watch out,' but she bustled towards the Cow Shed without a backward glance. He turned back to Janie. 'You OK?'

She nodded and rubbed her arm.

'Anyway, I'll let you get back to work. I'll pick you up around seven. We can have a drive out to a little place I know in Eskdale for a meal, OK?'

'Aye, lovely.' Watching him walk down the drive she felt like running after him but her first and foremost commitment was to the tearoom today. She rubbed her arm again where Kate had smashed into her. Her spell book came to mind.

Jess had witnessed the incident with Kate and Janie. It hadn't gone unnoticed by Mandy either. 'Did you see that?'

Jess nodded. 'I don't know why but she seems to have it in for Janie.'

'I think she wants her out the way for some reason.'

'Yeah, I think you're right. I'm going to have to say something when I get a minute.'

Mandy was enjoying the intrigue and busyness of the tearoom but suddenly thought she ought to go check on the twins. She found Keira in the garden on her own.

'Where's your sister?'

'I don't know.'

Mandy felt a tingle of panic prick her skin. She looked in the conservatory but Kirsty wasn't there. She checked in the loo. Not there either. She went to find Jess. 'Kirsty's gone missing, I'm gonna have to look for her.'

'Yeah, course. Probably in the loo.'

'No, looked in there.'

Jess saw Janie coming through from the tearoom. 'You seen Kirsty?'

Janie shook her head. 'She was in the garden last time I looked.'

Mandy whipped off her apron and ran outside. She stood looking all around, then decided to look for Kirsty where she'd found the twins on the day of Monika's wedding, in the donkey field. She hurried over there, hoping Kirsty hadn't taken it upon herself to wander any further. She tried not to think about that. Too many children went missing these days. The two donkeys were standing by the gate but no Kirsty. Mandy's heart plummeted. She climbed over the gate trying not to get stung by the nettles and hurried towards the old caravans, hoping Kirsty was playing in one of them. But no, not there either. Now Mandy was really panicking. Where else could she be? Hand at the level of her eyes, she scanned the field and beyond. A sudden movement took her eye. She picked her way across the deep-rutted mud baked by the sun, past the back gardens to the end one where she found Kirsty stroking a big tabby cat.

'There you are! What on earth d'you think you're doing? I've been looking everywhere for you!'

'Sorry Mum.'

Mandy blew out a sigh. 'Oh my God, how many times have I told you not to go wandering off? You're gonna have to stop reading those blasted Famous Five books.'

Kirsty started giggling.

'It's not funny, you nearly gave me a heart attack, come on.' But Mandy could see the funny side. She had to bite her lip.

Kirsty waved to the tabby. 'Bye-bye Gandy.'

'How do you know that cat's name?'

'He's Janie's cat. She told me.'

Mandy was processing this thought when she noticed a sun-tanned woman with a ponytail and a large backpack heading towards the kitchen door. Something about her looked familiar. Then she heard Jess's shout, 'Oh my God! Shelley!'

Mandy ran in and threw her arms round them both, all three in tears. Kirsty started jumping up and down. 'Auntie Shelley, Auntie Shelley!' and went to find her sister.

Eddie had heard the commotion too. Shelley turned to him. 'G'day, I don't think we've met?'

'Nope but I'm guessing you're Shelley, right?'

'Got it in one.'

'Hello, who's this?' asked Janie.

'Shelley, Jess's big sister. How you doin'?'

'Flat out at t' minute,' said Janie, turning to make another two coffees and cut some Victoria sponge.

Shelley looked at the twins. 'Wow! You've grown! And who are you?' she asked, looking at Eliot.

Jess picked him up. 'This is Eliot. Say hello to Auntie Shelley.' He started babbling.

Shelley took a moment. 'Geez, I forgot you'd had a sprog! '

They all laughed at this.

'Oh my God, it's so good to see you, Shel,' said Jess. 'It's been ages.'

Shelley looked sheepish. 'Yeah, sorry I didn't make it to your grand opening. Looks like you've got yourself a bonza place here, though.'

'Yeah thanks.' Jess saw Janie take another order and rush back in, 'but you've come at a really busy time. I'm gonna have to serve in a minute.'

'Take your sister into the lounge,' said Eddie, 'the three of us can look after things here.'

'Yeah, go ahead. We'll be fine,' said Mandy.

'Blimey,' said Shelley, 'you have got your hands full. Tell you what, why don't I take the kids up the swings?'

Jess plonked Eliot into Shelley's arms. 'You're not escaping that easily! Take him into the lounge while I get us a drink and you can tell me all about your travels.'

\*

Lydia Morgan was pacing the floor of her Greenwich apartment, the one she had once shared with Giles. It rankled that a nautical picture now hung in place of Coverdale. How dare Giles give it away; it was hers! The day she noticed it was missing she had stormed into his office and demanded he tell her where it was. 'I suppose you've auctioned it off? You always hated it!'

Giles had very calmly told her. 'No, I've given it to someone who appreciates it. All you see is pound signs, nothing to do with the art or the history behind it.'

Lydia's eyes had flashed. 'How dare you! I suppose it's that Blonde Tart you took up with. That painting has been in my family for generations.'

But Giles had played it down. 'And it still is. Look, we've been through all this; your family and hers are one and the same, get over it.'

She had stormed out of his office and had been scheming ever since.

Not only had the Blonde Tart got her grubby little paws on her painting but the worst thing was – between her, Giles and his father – they had found a way of swindling Lydia out of her great-grandfather's will. The Tart's Aussie sister was to blame of course, coming over here with the unlikely story of them being linked to Lydia's family. Huh! She was still seething when she thought about it. And on top of all that, last year, that same sister had had the gall to come here, in Greenwich, sniffing around looking for Giles!

A trickle of excitement now began to course through Lydia's veins. She had given Katherine an ultimatum hoping she wouldn't mess up this time. She was very disappointed in Katherine. Lydia was hoping for better progress by now but she was heartened by one encouraging thought – apparently the Tart's money was running out and her business was in difficulty. Ha! With a bit of luck she would soon be back where she belonged – in the gutter.

# TWENTY SEVEN

Jess clicked on her emails. There was one from a none-too-happy customer. She began to break out in a cold sweat as she read that their car had suffered damage to the shock absorbers. They thought they should warn Jess in case other guests sent her a bill for any damage. She needed to get the approach road repaired. *Oh my God! I knew I should've looked into getting that sorted.* She ran over to the workshop.

'Eddie, we've got a problem.'

He stopped polishing the Wolesley for the umpteenth time. 'What, another one?'

'It's that approach road. I've had an email from an unhappy customer – he's had to shell out loads on having his car repaired. Shock absorbers or something.'

'Christ, we can do without that.'

'Damn right. Luckily he's not sending us the bill but he's warned us that other customers might not be so amenable.'

'Bugger, I knew we should've done something about that. OK, I'll come in.' He hurriedly put the polish away and locked the workshop.

Eddie stared at the screen. 'Blimey, have you replied?'

'No, not yet.'

'Who owns that road anyway? Is it the council?'

Jess shook her head. 'No, I think it's old PJ. I bought the farmhouse from him, remember? I think we ought to check it out, though. We need to know where we stand.'

Jess glanced into the tearoom. It was stacked out with customers. Shelley had gone home with Mandy last night and was currently using their spare room. She was staying with the twins today to give Mandy the chance to work without worrying about them. Mandy and Janie had the tearoom covered but Jess went to make sure. 'Are you all right or shall I ring Shelley to come in and help? I just need to check on something. I might be a while.'

Mandy looked up from slicing a quiche. 'We're fine, Jess. Do what you have to.'

'I'll try not to be too long but if it gets too much, come and get me.' She took Eliot with her into the lounge and closed the door. She put him on the floor where he made straight for the sofa and hauled himself up, babbling away in his baby language.

Jess began to search through all the papers in the desk while Eddie went back over the old emails on his laptop. It was taking ages. Finally, Jess said, 'I'm losing the will, to be honest. I'll have to ring old PJ.'

Kate had been lurking while all this was going on. Yes! If the accounts were anything to go by and now the approach road was going to cost thousands, she might have some better news for Mrs Morgan. There was also the little matter of the painting to address. Kate saw her chance and tapped on the lounge door.

'Oh, hi Kate. Wassup?' said Jess.

'Nothing, I've been thinking… your lovely painting above the fireplace.'

'What about it?'

'Well, a few weeks back I couldn't help noticing how dark it was. It's a shame you can't see the detail. Maybe it would benefit from a professional clean? Ever thought of having it done?'

'To be honest, I haven't had time.'

'It would increase its value, you know.'

'OK, I'll look into it.' Eddie was still scrolling through the documents on his laptop. 'I've gotta go.' She went to close the door but Kate held it open.

'I know a very trustworthy restorer who can come and take a look, if you like?'

Jess was losing her patience. 'Yeah, OK, another time, Kate.'

Jess closed the door and Kate heard a key being turned in the lock. Damn! She hadn't handled that at all well.

*

Rudolf Pemberton-Jones was in his usual place staring out the French windows when the phone shrilled. Damn and blast! Who the hell could that be?

Jess tried to get all her facts straight. 'Mr P...er...Pemberton-Jones?' she corrected herself just in time. 'Hello, Jess Harvey here. Am I right in thinking you own the approach road to Bracken Farmhouse?'

Good God, now what? Rosemary dealt with all this stuff, but she was out as usual. 'Why?'

'I've had an email from a customer saying the potholes have caused damage to his suspension. I need to know who's responsible for that road.'

He blew out a sigh. 'I see. I'll look into it and let you know. I think there's a covenant in place.'

'What's a covenant?'

'I'm not going into all that now. I'll get my wife to phone you.' He slammed the phone down and poured himself another glass of single malt.

*

Giles put the phone down after speaking to Laura. Not only did she need his services for the lease but now her husband was divorcing her. He was deep in thought when Gloria buzzed his intercom. 'Ms Harvey's on the phone for you, Mr Morgan.'

'Oh? Put her through would you?'

'Hi, Giles, how are you?'

He instantly brightened. 'Fine, thanks. Nice to hear from you. How's the business going?'

'It's going great, we're really busy, but I was wondering if I could ask your advice on something?'

'Fire away.'

Jess took a breath. 'I don't know if you remember but there's an approach road to the farmhouse?'

'Er…yes.'

'Well, I need to know who's responsible for that road and I can't find anything in my deeds.'

'Right, refresh my memory. Who owns that road?'

'That's just it, I don't know, but it's in a bit of a state and I don't want my customers suing me.' She didn't want to tell him about the email.

'OK leave it with me. I'll look into it and get back to you.'

'Thanks.'

'Before you go, I understand you've had a Laura Dean staying with you? She's leasing an old shop in the village, is that right?'

'Yes, I gave her your name. I hope you didn't mind?'

'No not at all. I might have to go up to the Dales and pay her a visit at some point.'

'Cool, you could drop in on us, as well!'

'I'll look forward to it. I'll be in touch… about the covenant.'

'Thanks Giles.'

He put the phone down and asked Gloria to make an open-ended reservation at the Park Hotel in Harrogate.

*

Carol stepped off the train and spotted her son-in-law heading towards her. Trevor greeted her with a flashing smile and a kiss on her cheek. She could see why her daughter had fallen for him.

'Let me take that,' said Trevor, taking her case. 'How was the journey?'

'Hot! I'm looking forward to a nice shower.'

As Carol sat in the passenger seat the twins popped their heads up in the back. 'Hello Grandma!'

'Oh, what a lovely surprise! I didn't expect to see you till we got back to the house.' Carol fished in her handbag and gave them each a packet of sweets. 'Here you are, just a little something, don't eat them all at once.'

Their eyes lit up. 'Ooh, thanks Grandma!' Mandy very rarely let them have sweets and Kirsty immediately ripped her packet open sending some of the M&Ms to the floor. She scrabbled around behind Trevor's seat trying to pick them up.

'You can't eat them now,' said Keira. 'They'll be all dirty.'

But Kirsty stuffed one in her mouth and pulled a face at her sister.

Mandy hummed to herself in the kitchen. She had prepared a chicken salad and put a bottle of white wine on ice, hoping to make the most of eating al fresco on this warm evening. She was hoping to include Shelley in the family gathering but she'd gone round to Jess and Eddie's, saying she'd sleep on the sofa, leaving Mandy's spare room free for Carol.

The twins burst in through the door with Carol and Trevor. Mandy hugged her mum. 'Oh, it's so good to see you.' She clocked Kirsty, 'Hey, I hope you're not eating those before dinner?'

'See, told you!' said Keira and turned to Mandy with a smug grin. 'I'm saving mine.'

'All right, you two. Go and wash your hands. Dinner won't be long.'

*

Janie was home after a sublime evening with Darren. He'd taken her to a cosy little pub in the heart of the Dales where they'd enjoyed a delicious meal sitting in candlelight. He had surprised her by saying he had always meant to explore spiritualism and metaphysics and they'd had a stimulating discussion. Every time she saw Darren he had the most tantalising effect on her and she hoped this episode wasn't going to be a one-off. She wanted him. She hoped he felt the same about her, but she was disappointed when he dropped her off saying he had to pack and leave early in the morning.

Trying to put her restless energy to good use, Janie decided to do something positive, something she'd been meaning to do for a while. She lit her candles and her incense, sat cross-legged on the rug and tried to concentrate. This wasn't easy when all she could think of was how Darren had looked into her eyes and made her feel when he kissed her. At long last her life was taking a turn for the better but there was one person who didn't fit into it right now and she was going to have to do something about her. Nothing nasty, for she knew it was unethical and morally wrong to use her magic that way, but she had decided some time ago to make everyone's life easier where Kate was concerned. She put herself into calm mode, took out her book of spells, thumbed through to find the appropriate page and ushered her incantation.

She was interrupted by a knock at the door. She quickly put her spell book away. Knowing how difficult it had been to concentrate she hoped her spell hadn't gone awry; she didn't want Kate on her doorstep. She tentatively opened the door to see Darren standing in the moonlight. Her heart filled as he whisked her off her feet and kissed her.

'It won't matter if I'm a bit late tomorrow. I just had to come back.'

*

It turned out that Shelley had gone to South America after leaving Giles in La Rochelle two years ago, that's why she hadn't come to Jess and Eddie's grand opening. She had got hooked up with a group of Aussies who planned to make their way to Peru. That was Shelley all over, always looking for the next adventure and her feet were already starting to itch but, knowing Jess would be disappointed if she did a disappearing act so soon, she had decided to stay a bit longer and help out in the tearoom today.

Shelley had noticed the cleaner who had collected her gear and made a quick exit just now. There was something about her. Where had she seen those shifty movements before? After travelling over much of the globe there were only a handful of people that stood out in her memory, but this woman definitely plucked at her recall strings.

'You alright there, Shel?' asked Jess, noticing her puzzled expression.

Shelley scratched her head. 'Er, yeah...who's your cleaner?'

'What, the one that's just gone through?'

Shelly nodded. 'I dunno but there's something familiar about her. Maybe it's just my mind playing tricks.'

Jess frowned. 'Maybe. I don't know where you'd have seen her.'

Shelley shook her head. 'Nope, I'm sure I've seen her somewhere. Has she always lived here?'

'No, she lived in London before she moved up here. I think she used to work for a cleaning agency in Greenwich.'

Shelley clicked her fingers. 'That's it!'

'What is?'

'Last year, I had a couple of weeks spare before setting off again and thought I'd call in at Giles's apartment and surprise him.'

Jess nodded. 'And?'

'I was the one who got the surprise! It turned out that Giles's apartment now belongs to Cruella. I think it was your cleaner that opened the door to me.'

Jess's eyes were on stalks. 'What? Oh. My. God!' Jess sat down, her mind busily trying to make the connections. 'I knew there was something fishy going on. So, did you see The Wicked Witch?'

'No, thank God, she was in France apparently, but I'm sure my visit would've gotten back to her.'

'Right, that does it!' Jess marched over to the workshop to tell Eddie. 'You'll never guess...' She shook her head, incredulous. 'Huh, I can't believe the lengths that woman will go to!'

'What are you on about?'

'It turns out that Kate is Lydia's spy!'

Eddie looked nonplussed.

'Cruella, Giles's ex, remember? Kate's working for her!'

'Blimey! How d'you know?'

'Shelley just recognised her. She bumped into her in Greenwich last year. She went to what she thought was Giles's apartment. It turned out that Lydia lives there now, when she's not in France, and it was Kate who opened the bloody door to her!'

Eddie nodded. 'Christ, and she's been trying to get into our accounts!'

Jess felt sick. To think she could've been on the brink of losing everything she'd ever worked for. She didn't know how she hadn't sussed it before but it was obvious now she thought about it. All those incidents, the sneakiness, the hanging around and the terrible way she'd treated Janie. Of course!

Jess made her way upstairs to find Kate. There was something she should've done a long time ago.

# TWENTY EIGHT

Jess, Mandy and Ramona sat in the gleaming Buick Roadster with its hood down feeling like movie stars.

'Wow!' said Ramona, 'this is well cool! '

Mandy agreed, 'Yeah, it really is.'

Jess felt very proud sitting next to Eddie but she was worried about the potholes. 'Watch out!' she cried, 'the worst one's up ahead.'

'I'm on it,' said Eddie. He didn't want a puncture or worse; that would certainly blow his chances.

Jess had closed Jessica's Parlour for the day. Carol was in charge of the kids while Janie was giving the kitchen a long-overdue deep clean. Normally this job would've fallen to Kate but Jess had fired her and asked her other cleaner, Sue, to help Janie today. Jess was still coming to terms with the fact that Lydia had gone to all the trouble of getting Kate to do her dirty work. She was thankful that Shelley had arrived when she did, otherwise she hated to think what could've happened. Shelley had been dossing down in Jess's lounge for the past few nights. She knew Shelley was a late riser and, not wanting to disturb her, Jess had left her there this morning.

Eddie drove through the wrought iron gates of Thornwood Manor like he owned the place and parked in the old stable yard to wait for Guy. Jess, Mandy and Ramona hopped out and followed the arrows directing the extras along the path to the back of the manor where people were milling around in the courtyard with cups of coffee. In the wood-panelled anti-room there was an overbearing smell of hot fried food and people were helping themselves from the trays set out on trestle tables all along one side of the room.

'Let's go grab some,' said Ramona, joining the queue.

Remembering what her mum had told her, Mandy followed. 'Come on Jess. We might not get another chance.'

Jess turned up her nose. It wasn't a patch on what she offered her guests, but she took heed of Mandy's advice and helped herself to a plate of bacon, sausages and tomatoes and two slices of toast. She went to find Mandy and Ramona, who, having squeezed on the end of one of the tables, budged up to let Jess sit down. The extras had been told they would be provided with 1950s costumes at the venue and some people were already kitted out. Through another door Jess caught a glimpse of a few women sitting in front of illuminated mirrors having their make-up applied and their hair done. While she ate Jess noticed Kate running in and out with huge tea and coffee pots.

'Blimey!' whispered Jess, 'don't look now but it looks like Lydia's puppet has got herself another job.'

Mandy took a sneak peek and raised her eyebrows.

The food demolished they poured themselves a hot drink from the pots on the table. Kate had made herself scarce. Jess couldn't believe she had the gall to show her face after what had happened.

There didn't seem to be anything happening. The place was quiet. No one came to tell them the order of the proceedings and there was no one to ask. Jess, Mandy and Ramona were getting fidgety. Then the woman who had been taking the photos at the auditions came to check their details. 'That's all in order. When you're ready, go to wardrobe and select your outfits.'

'Come on, then,' said Jess. 'Let's do it.'

In the adjoining room stood rails of clothes; shoes and handbags littered the floor. People were grabbing what they could and going into a makeshift changing room with a shabby curtain pulled across.

Mandy held up a few garments. 'Really? I've seen better in Oxfam.'

'It's all crap,' said Ramona, going through the racks, 'and I can't find any in my size.'

They rummaged around until a woman sprang from nowhere, stopped and stared at Jess. 'Oh, now I think I've got the very thing for you!' She walked to the end of the rail and produced a pale blue two-piece. 'Come here darling. What size are you?'

'Twelve,' said Jess.

She held the outfit against Jess, 'Perfect! Go and try.' She shoved it at Jess and turned to Mandy. 'Mm, burgundy hair. Ooh, I know.' She pulled out a bright green dress and bolero and held it against Mandy. 'Yup, that'll do you darling. Off you go.'

That left Ramona. The woman looked her up and down. 'Size?'

Ramona breathed in. 'Fourteen.'

The woman searched along the rail and pulled out a bright pink off-the-shoulder dress with a nipped-in waist.

'I ain't wearing that! I hate pink.'

'Nonsense, you'll look fab darling, what with your dark hair and up against your friends…perfect. When you're done pop along to make-up.'

Ramona snatched the dress and stormed off to get changed. She struggled into the pink dress feeling like a tube of toothpaste squeezed in the middle.

All three finally looked each other up and down.

'Could be worse I suppose,' said Mandy, adjusting the shoulders on her green outfit.

'You look cool,' said Jess.

'I'm screwed,' said Ramona, folding her arms across her chest.

'Yeah, you're right,' said Jess. 'Come on, let's find you something else *darling*.' They broke into giggles.

Eventually Ramona emerged from the changing room in a black dress and jacket looking very demure.

'Fab, *darling*,' sniggered Mandy, and they all headed for the make-up room.

Having been told to keep a low profile Eddie stood watching the action from inside the doorway of one of the old stables. It had taken a lot longer than he'd thought, so much hanging around, and they seemed to be shooting the film in a very strange order. But at least they had plied him with his own pot of coffee and a bacon butty.

Eddie was suddenly alert as a dark-haired actor, looking for all the world like Gregory Peck, got into the Buick and drove along the carriage drive and up to the manor. Eddie was chuffed to bits to see his pride and joy being used. He couldn't wait to see her on the big screen! She looked the business. He watched as the actor slammed the car door and waited in the porch until another actor emerged dressed like a butler and showed him inside. Two more takes then another actor got into the black Wolseley, now complete with its police sign on the grid, drove it up to the manor and parked behind the Buick. This time a row ensued between two actors standing on the porch before going inside. Next a man dressed in a brown tweed suit, hair swept back, sat in the beige Austin but the engine wouldn't turn over.

'Cut!' shouted the cameraman.

Eddie rushed over to the Austin. Tristan emerged. 'Well, this is embarrassing. I thought you said these cars were up to the mark?'

'I'll sort it, don't worry, it's only something minor.' With clammy hands Eddie fiddled about under the bonnet until he found the problem. The Austin finally burst into life and Eddie heaved a sigh of relief.

At lunchtime Eddie was treated to smoked salmon and avocado salad with a glass of prosecco, sitting with Guy and Tristan in the old stable yard bathed in sunshine. Eddie kept apologising for the glitch with the Austin but Guy waved it away. 'Don't feel bad. These things are bound to happen with old cars.' He slapped Eddie on the back. 'Glad to have you on board,' and lifted his glass to toast him. 'Cheers!'

But no such luck for Jess, Mandy or Ramona. Their day was dragging. The young make-up artists were more interested in chatting than getting the job done. Jess's thoughts turned to Eliot, of all the things she could be doing at home and all the customers she had turned away.

'Here, come on,' said Mandy. 'I'm not hanging around any longer.' She marched up to one of the dressing tables and began to help herself to the make-up trays. Jess joined her.

The young make-up artists glared at them but said nothing. One woman strode up to Mandy. 'Good idea, love. Let's get on with it, I've been waiting ages.'

'Budge up,' said Ramona, and squeezed into the tiny space for Jess to get to work on her.

Job done, they gave each other a high five and went back to the anti-room to wait for the next stage of the proceedings. They waited. And they waited. Suddenly the woman who had been in charge of costume shot out from behind the scenes and took a group of extras into the depths of the manor.

'I wonder when it's our turn,' said Ramona. 'No one seems to be going outside for the garden party scene or anything, and I'm starving.'

Just then the costumes woman came back and gave the nod to another two women standing near the door. Apparently, they had been waiting for the sun to come out. 'OK, all outside. Take a glass of lemonade from the table, pretend it's prosecco, and assemble in groups of twos or threes. You're at a high society gathering. Act natural and chat amongst yourselves. And do try to look as if you're enjoying it!'

Jess, Mandy and Ramona edged towards the table near the door laid out with glasses of fake sparkling wine. Jess clocked Kate helping to pour the drinks, but she kept her head down. Jess downed her glass and took another.

'Only one each!' shouted the woman.

Mandy downed hers and said to Kate, 'Quick, give us another, I'm gasping.'

But Kate ignored her. Mandy snatched another glass anyway, so did Ramona. They followed Jess out into the sun-drenched courtyard where some of the men looked the part in their dinner suits accompanied by women looking very stylish with hats and long gloves and a few in fur stoles.

'Hey, how come they've had special treatment?' complained Mandy.

'Maybe they brought their own,' said Ramona.

There was no sign of the cameraman or anyone who looked remotely like a director. 'I'm going back in to find a hat,' said Jess.

Mandy and Ramona looked horrified. 'You'll miss all the action!' said Mandy, but Jess ran inside and found a large-brimmed white hat and plonked it on her head, winked at her image in the mirror and ran back to the courtyard to stand with the others. Just in time. The jaws of the black and white clapperboard snapped shut and the cameras began to roll. The director called for two more takes and then the dark clouds blotted out the sun.

'Don't like the look of that,' said Jess, looking up at the sky and edging closer to the door. Mandy and Ramona followed her. Just in time for a bolt of lightning split the sky and down came the rain. A few women shrieked and barged past them and into the anti-room.

'Here, don't mind us!' shouted Mandy, rubbing her arm.

In strutted the wardrobe woman looking very officious and told them to take off their clothes and hang them back on the rack. Filming was finished for the day. 'Listen up,' she shouted, trying to make herself heard above the din, 'we might want you again tomorrow so don't make any arrangements.'

'How will we know?' shouted someone.

'You'll get a text.'

Outside the old stables, Eddie was quickly fastening the hood on the Buick. Guy came running up to him. 'Want a hand?'

'Thanks mate.'

Once the hood was secured Eddie sat in the car watching the rain bouncing off the bonnet. Tristan jumped in beside him, brushing the rain off his hair. 'Christ! Bloody weather. Your cars look amazing by the way. I haven't had a chance to tell you, but Guy thinks we got some great shots.'

'Awesome. I still need to do a bit of work on the Austin, though.'

'No worries, all good.' Guy patted the walnut dashboard. 'We'll need this little beauty again tomorrow, weather permitting of course, and the police car.'

'Sure. You've got my number.'

After dropping Ramona home, Eddie, Jess and Mandy piled into the kitchen and headed for the drinks machine.

'How was it?' asked Carol.

'I think you know the answer to that, Mum,' smirked Mandy.

'Well, I did warn you.'

'Eddie got the best deal,' said Jess. 'Smoked salmon and avocado salad, jammy bugger!'

Eddie looked smug. 'I can't help it. I thought you'd all had the same.'

'Huh, fat chance,' said Mandy. 'Twins OK?'

'Yes,' said Carol. 'I made sure they didn't wander off.

'

Janie came through from the conservatory with the twins. 'We had a walk up the swings earlier,' she said, squeezing Eliot's chubby leg. 'He loved it.'

Jess took Eliot from her and showered him with kisses. 'Ooh, I've missed you. Have you been a good boy?'

'He's no trouble,' said Carol. 'He's had his bath and I was just about to give him his tea. We've had a nice day, haven't we Janie?'

She nodded and sat down. 'Aye, fun but exhausting!'

Jess looked around. 'Where's Shelley?'

Janie and Carol looked at each other. 'She left shortly after you,' said Janie, 'said she was going to explore the moors and camp out under the stars for a couple of nights.'

'What?' Jess unlocked the lounge door to find all Shelley's things were gone. She sighed, 'She could've waited and said goodbye.' But Jess had been half expecting it. Shelley could never stick around for long.

'Oh,' said Carol, 'I nearly forgot – there was a man, said he was a restorer or something, came to take a look at the oil painting, Jess. I didn't know where Shelley had left the key so I couldn't show him in. He said he'd be in touch.'

Jess frowned. 'Mm, that's funny – I haven't asked anyone...'

'Well, he seemed to know all about it.'

# TWENTY NINE

Jess's phone woke her up. *Oh my God! What time is it?* She could hear Eddie downstairs feeding Eliot. She bounced out of bed and swiped the green button.

'Good morning,' said Giles, 'I've looked into the land registry and there appears to be a covenant.'

Jess tried to get her head together. 'Sorry, can you explain what that actually means?'

'Yes, basically it means that although Mr Pemberton-Jones still owns the road, you, the new owner of Bracken Farmhouse, are responsible for any repairs.'

'No! Oh my God!'

'Yes, quite. It could run into thousands.'

'I hope not. Isn't there a way round it?'

She heard Giles blow out his cheeks. 'There might be. I could ask Mr Pemberton-Jones if he's willing to come to some arrangement.'

'What? Like go halves, you mean?'

'Yes.'

'Well, good luck with that! He's always pleading poverty and putting his rents up.'

'Right, leave it with me. I'm sure there's something we can do.'

'Thanks Giles.' She liked that he said *we*. She ran downstairs to tell Eddie what Giles had said. 'It might not be so bad. How much we got in the kitty?'

'I'm not sure, I'll have a look.' He unlocked the lounge door and opened his laptop.

Jess took Eliot out of his highchair, followed Eddie and shut the door. Eddie was frowning, clicking and searching, going back over the emails.

'Wassup?' Jess put Eliot down and went to look. 'Oh my God! What's that?' She pointed to the screen.

'A final council tax demand.' He turned to the oil painting above the fireplace. 'We can always sell that.'

'You leave my painting alone! It's not going anywhere.'

'Well, if we need the money…it doesn't exactly go in here anyway.'

'Oh my God, it wasn't you that asked that restorer to come round, was it?'

'No! Course not.'

Jess blew out her cheeks. 'If you hadn't been pissing about with those old wrecks…'

Eddie shook his head in dismay. 'What? That's got nothing to do with it. That money comes out of my personal account, you know that! It's not my fault we're overdrawn. You should've have been keeping an eye on the accounts.'

'I haven't had time!'

At their raised voices Eliot started crying. Jess picked him up and kissed him. 'It's all right sweetheart, don't cry.' Her phone pinged. 'Blimey, they need us up at the manor in an hour! We'll have to sort this lot out later.'

Eddie was still scrolling. 'What? Oh yeah, they'll need the Wolesley as well. Is Carol on stand-by?'

'Yes, and Janie's coming in. Oh my God, I can't shut the tearoom again today; we need all the money we can get.'

*

As soon as Giles ended the call to Jess, another came in. It put a huge smile on his face.

'Hello Giles. Can I come and see you?'

'Yes, of course. Problems with the lease?'

'Not exactly. My husband is divorcing me and I'd like you to act for me.'

Giles felt a spike of excitement. He could act on Laura's behalf for both the shop *and* her divorce, but he would have to be careful. He didn't want to be named as co-respondent. Laura had told him what her husband was like, and he could do without that kind of trouble. 'Yes, I don't see why not. You'll have to give me the name of your husband's solicitor and the details.'

'Thanks Giles. I'll bring them with me.'

'On second thoughts, can you email them to me instead, along with any correspondence? Then I can get to work on it straight away.'

'Yes, if you'd rather.'

'Thanks. I'll be in touch.' He smiled smugly. He'd got out of that one very nicely.

*

Kate smirked when she saw Jess, Mandy and Ramona rush into the anti-room at the manor. Now, if *she* had been chosen for an extra she'd have been first in every day. She had organised the drinks in advance hoping for a quick exit when filming started. She needed to make a couple of phone calls and earn some much-needed brownie points.

People were frantically looking for their costumes from yesterday. Jess and Mandy quickly found theirs and got changed. Ramona's black dress had been kicked into a dusty corner. 'Bloody typical! Why is it always me?' She picked it up and hastily brushed off the cobwebs.

Mandy poked her head round the door of the make-up room. There was no sign of the girls and the room was in darkness. 'Looks like it's down to us today then, Jess.'

'No probs. We'll do a better job anyway. Hopefully there won't be so much hanging around either. I need to get back.'

Mandy gave Jess one of her looks. 'Everything all right? You seem a bit stressed.'

'Oh, it's nothing. I'll sort it.' She didn't want to tell Mandy her stomach was churning at the thought of being overdrawn. She had always prided herself on her financial management. Also, she didn't want to mention that she'd argued with Eddie but it was bugging her. How could he suggest she sell her painting of Coverdale? Didn't he know how much that piece of family history meant to her?

'I'm here for you, Jess. You know that. If there's anything I can do…'

'Thanks, I know.'

Mandy gave her a hug and Ramona noticed. 'You guys OK?'

'Yeah, fine,' said Jess. 'Come on, let's do this.'

\*

Eddie wasn't needed in the afternoon. He went straight home intending to get onto the accounts. He couldn't believe Jess had accused him of using her money to restore his cars! They very rarely rowed about anything and he didn't like where this was going.

There was a lull in the tearoom. Carol had taken Eliot and the twins up to the swings. He checked Janie didn't need him, made a coffee and took it into the lounge. The sun was hitting the painting of Coverdale showing up the sleeping figure beneath the tree. He supposed it wasn't that bad really. If only Giles hadn't given it to Jess. They had enough on their plate without worrying about the painting.

His brain cogs began to turn as he scrolled through the debits again. Knowing that Kate had been working for Mrs Morgan he wanted to make sure he hadn't missed any dodgy outgoings. He smiled at Jess's names for her, The Wicked Witch, The Bitch from Hell and Cruella, but this was no laughing matter. However, the accounts were in a mess and he was thankful that Trevor would soon be taking over the financial reins leaving Jess free to do what she did best and Eddie to concentrate on his cars. But what if they had to cough up for the repairs to the approach road? He preferred not to think about that.

Back at the manor, things were looking up. The staff had served up a delicious lunch of spicy chicken and wild rice with poppadums along with a veggie alternative that put a smile on Ramona's face. They were stacking their dirty plates when all the extras were called to assemble in the courtyard.

'Have I got food round me mouth?' asked Ramona.

'Nope, you're good,' said Jess. 'Have I?'

Mandy shook her head. 'I need to refresh my lipstick though.' She rushed back to the make-up room and did a double take. Kate was sneakily applying some make-up and wearing a bright pink dress and heels. Mandy rushed back out to find Jess and Ramona queuing up for their drinks.

Jess looked around. 'No Kate today?'

'No,' said Mandy. 'She was in the make-up room all dolled up!'

Jess's eyes widened. 'Really?'

Mandy nodded. There was no time to explain. All the extras were being hustled out to the courtyard. Jess, Mandy and Ramona pushed their way into the crowd. *Snap* went the clapperboard and the cameras began to roll, then everyone turned to stare at a waitress barging through the partygoers searching for someone. She found the woman she was looking for and dragged her back to the house like a naughty child. Jess and Mandy were agog. It was Kate.

'Cut!' shouted the director.

Everyone groaned. Ramona started giggling. 'Blimey! Looks like she's about to kill her!'

'Well, it is a murder mystery!' said Jess.

'I reckon she'd be doing you a favour,' said Mandy.

'Yeah, especially since she's been snooping around in our accounts.'

'Oh my God!' said Mandy. 'I knew there was something fishy about her.'

Ramona's eyes were twice their size. 'She's been what?'

'Yeah, I'll tell you later.' Jess's stomach turned over, wondering how much Kate actually knew about their finances. She also suspected it was Kate who'd asked the so-called restorer to call yesterday knowing they would be out of the house. The Bitch from Hell was behind it, of course. Not only had she used Kate to do her snooping, but it now seemed she would stop at nothing to get her hands on Coverdale. Thank God Shelley had locked the door before she left!

The cameras were getting into position again and everyone was told to settle down. This time the filming went according to plan. After another three takes all the extras were told to de-robe and to each collect an envelope on their way out.

Mandy ripped hers open. 'Fifty quid! Is that all?'

'Still, better than a poke in the eye,' said Ramona.

Jess thought she would need a lot more than fifty quid to get her out of trouble.

*

Lydia was fuming. Mr Gambol had been unable to gain access to the painting of Coverdale and now Katherine, the stupid woman, had delusions of becoming an actress! Whatever next? This was all getting too much. And there was no point in getting Mr Gambol to try again; they would surely smell a rat. She was tempted to shog off back to

France and forget the whole thing, but she still wanted to get even with the Blonde Tart. Think, Goddammit! Think!

# THIRTY

Rosemary Pemberton-Jones was in a flap. She'd opened a letter this morning from Giles Morgan of Morgan Bishop solicitors, asking Mr Pemberton-Jones to confirm that he owned the approach road to Bracken Farmhouse. If this was the case, he was liable for any repairs. Apparently, this uncertainty had been brought to Ms Harvey's notice as one of her customers had experienced some damage to their vehicle. Rosemary was frantically searching through all the drawers for the documents when Rudolf came into the estate office.

'What on earth are you doing, woman?' She ignored him and continued rummaging. Rudolf stilled her hand. 'What are you looking for?'

'The land registry documents... didn't we change the deeds when we sold Bracken Farmhouse? Wasn't there a covenant?'

Rudolf felt hot under the collar. He had told Ms Harvey that this was indeed the case but, now he thought about it, he didn't know if he'd added the covenant or not. 'I...I can't remember.'

'What do you mean, you can't remember? You silly old fool! Our solicitor should know. Get Soames onto it!'

'The deeds aren't here, anyway. They're locked away in the bank vault.'

'Well, you'd better find out how we stand. I knew we shouldn't have sold the farmhouse to that woman! She's been nothing but trouble from day one; seeking planning permission for this and that...'

Rudolf zoned out. He hadn't said anything to Rosemary but he thought deep down that Ms Harvey had done an excellent job on the derelict farmhouse. Just a pity he hadn't leased it to her instead of selling it. It was rather short-sighted of him.

*

Laura was pleased with her new décor in the flat. Wanting to create a coastal feel she'd used crisp blue and white striped bedlinen, hung a seascape above the bed and placed a model yacht on the chest of drawers.

To add a little colour in the otherwise stark white kitchen she'd placed a vase of assorted sweet peas on the granite worktop. Filled with nervous anticipation she breathed in their fresh fragrance and set a tea tray with her delicate china and two slices of lemon drizzle cake from the village bakery.

The shop front was now forest green with a newly glazed window and door, the name Rain or Shine in gold lettering above. Very stylish, thought Giles as he rang the doorbell. Laura raced down the stairs and greeted him with a broad smile.

*

Carol had had a wonderful fortnight with Mandy, Trevor and the twins and was now, back home, feeling very lonely. The house was deathly quiet apart from the traffic thundering past her door, the noise brought more keenly to her notice after staying in the peaceful Dales village. Mandy, Trevor and the twins were waiting to move into the barn conversion and Carol was looking forward to moving into the annexe, a hop across from Mandy's doors. What was there here for her, anyway? Oh, she had June next door, but she sometimes felt like a hanger-on. She didn't want to encroach on other peoples' families.

Trying to find something to do to take her mind off the emptiness she was feeling, she went upstairs to turn out some cupboards ready for when she moved. Years of hoarding fell out when she opened the wardrobe in the spare room. None of it was worth very much – old lamp shades, faded bedlinen, outdated clothes. The best bits would have to go to the charity shops and the rest to the tip. She didn't know why she'd kept it all but as she started going through the items, they all presented her with memories. The dinner dances at Barry's workplace, the holidays. Before she knew it two hours had passed.

She was just about to put it all back and make a cuppa when she saw the big box of photos on the floor of the wardrobe. She knelt down and lifted the lid to see Mandy at sixteen smiling back at her, her darling girl. Where had those years gone? So much had happened during that time – Mandy and Trevor's mixed-race wedding, and Barry, such a proud Dad walking her down the aisle. Carol smiled at the new-born twins' photo; how cute they were. She had loved watching them grow, every little antic, and how different they were in temperament! They were now looking forward to starting their new school and making new friends and Carol was eager for all their news. She missed them already. She squashed down the lump in her throat and went to put the kettle on.

*

Jess was walking back from Ramona's with Eliot in his buggy when her mobile rang. 'Hi, Giles, how are you?'

'I'm great thanks. I'm calling with some good news. Your approach road problem has been resolved. The Pemberton-Jones's have confirmed that the repairs are down to them.'

'Oh wow! That's brilliant, thanks Giles.'

'Yes, I thought you'd be pleased.'

'Pleased? I'm over the moon. But hang on, what happened to the covenant thing?'

'Don't worry about that. I've dealt with it.'

'Awesome! So, what happens now? When will they start the repairs?'

'As soon as possible. It's in the Pemberton-Jones's own interests anyway; they won't want to be sued for any damage. In the meantime, I have suggested the highways agency erect some warning signs at the entrance to the road.'

'Cool. Thanks Giles.'

'You're welcome.'

Jess hurried home to give Eddie the good news. He was in his usual place putting some finishing touches to the Austin. He'd had some more work pass his way; another film company that InPictures had put him in touch with and filming would begin at the end of the year. He looked round when he heard the buggy on the gravel. 'Hiya, had a good time?'

Jess beamed. 'Guess what?'

Eddie shook his head.

'The repairs to the approach road are down to the PJs! Giles has just rung.'

'Oh, fantastic! Trevor's been on – he's looking forward to starting next week.'

'Brilliant!' Jess threw her arms round Eddie and kissed him.

'Hey, watch out! I'm all oily.'

She dropped her arms. 'I'm sorry if I've been a bit of a bitch lately.'

'You're all right.'

Eliot was making impatient noises and rocking the buggy towards the kitchen door.

Jess laughed. 'I think he wants his lunch.'

'I know how he feels,' said Eddie. He wiped his hands on a rag, patted the Austin's bonnet and closed the workshop.

Mandy and Janie were chatting at the table.

'Everything all right?' asked Jess.

'Yeah, all good,' said Mandy. 'We were just grabbing a coffee.'

Janie looked at the kitchen clock and jumped up to put on her coat.

'Got a bus to catch?' said Eddie.

Janie smiled. 'Darren's back from t' Orkneys – he's taking me out this afternoon.' She turned to Jess. 'If you don't need me in here?'

'No, go ahead.'

'Very nice, too,' said Eddie. He winked, 'have fun!'

\*

Mandy and Trevor were finally moving into their barn conversion. They had hired a van and Eddie had volunteered to help with moving the furniture. They had made a good team and they had it all done in no time.

Last but not least, Mandy drove Jess's old Pink Peril back to the rental with the twins to fetch the cats. Sylvester was in the kitchen, so she quickly scooped him up and put him in the car. No such luck with Buster. They searched all the rooms but he was nowhere to be seen. 'If he doesn't show up we'll have come back tomorrow,' said Mandy.

Kirsty started crying, 'We can't leave him here. It's not fair.' She went to the kitchen door and called his name. After a few minutes he jumped over the fence and ran up to her meowing. She picked him up and buried her face in his soft fur. 'Honestly, what are you like?'

Mandy had to smile. 'He's a good match for you!'

When both cats were installed in their new home they looked very put out at having to get used to another abode. Buster sniffed all around the kitchen while Sylvester sat by the bi-fold doors grumpily looking out.

'Will they be all right?' asked Keira.

'Yeah, they'll soon get used to it,' said Mandy. 'We'll keep them in for the first week like we did before and, anyway, we haven't got far to go back for them if they wander back to the other house. And it's a quiet road.' She left them and went to inspect the rooms with all their furniture in place.

Trevor found her in the lounge looking through the window at the view. 'Happy?'

She smiled and hugged him. 'Mm, very.'

'Eddie's gone back for Jess and Eliot.' He held up a bottle of champagne. 'Thought we'd christen the new house.'

'Ooh, I love you, Trevor King.'

'Love you too, Mandy King.' He kissed her. 'This'll be the making of us.'

# THIRTY ONE

Giles drove his silver Mercedes S class carefully along the approach road. He could see what all the fuss was about – there were some rather deep potholes and he hoped it wouldn't be too long before the road was repaired.

He parked up and scanned the area. He hadn't realised the complex was so big but, from where he stood, it looked as if Jessica had done an excellent job. His heart did a little flip remembering how he'd met her and where she'd come from. He felt inexplicably happy for her.

As he stood in the porch he noticed the well-kept tea garden. There were some winter pansies in the window boxes which he assumed would've been full of annuals during the summer months and he approved of the way the ferns and moss curled around the stonework. In fact, his parents' place came to mind and he smiled at his memory of the dinner party that Jess and her friend had inadvertently stumbled upon and the pleasurable hour with Jessica in the summerhouse that had led to his divorce. Yes, he was glad to be rid of Lydia.

Jess opened the door, a big smile on her face. 'Hi Giles! Lovely to see you, come in.'

He was thankful she didn't have the child with her; he wasn't in the mood for idle baby-talk. 'Thanks. I had a quick look around outside – you've done an excellent job.'

'Thanks.' She was unsure whether to give him a hug, but she did anyway. He responded with a quick peck on her cheek.

'Come through. We're in the lounge.'

Feeling slightly uncomfortable, Eddie jumped up as soon as Giles entered. They shook hands.

'Good to see you,' said Eddie. 'Have a seat. Drink?'

Giles glanced at his Rolex. 'Er, I don't want to encroach on your evening and I'm driving to Harrogate later.' It wasn't a lie – he hoped to call in on Laura and take her back to his hotel.

'No problem,' said Jess. 'Can I get you a cup of tea? Earl Grey?'

Giles smiled. 'Perfect.'

'I'll get it,' said Eddie, not wanting to be left in the room with his old adversary.

Giles sat on the edge of the pale blue armchair and looked around. 'Very nice.'

'Thanks, a bit different to Peckham!'

He smiled, not quite sure what to talk about. He settled for, 'I understand you have a child, a little boy, is that right?'

'Yeah, Eliot, he's nearly a year old. Huh, I don't know where the time goes. He's upstairs in his cot – sleeps the clock round!' She gave a self-conscious giggle. She jumped up and proudly showed Giles a photo of her blond son.

He glanced at it. 'And you're happy?'

Jess nodded and flashed her engagement ring.

'I'm pleased for you.'

'Thanks.'

'When's the big day?'

'We've booked Thornwood Manor for next June. You'll get an invite.'

His eyes strayed to the painting above the fireplace. 'Ah, back home, where it belongs.'

Jess walked over to the picture in its heavy guilt frame. 'Yes, but there's been something funny going on.'

'Oh?'

'There was a so-called restorer last week, came when we were out, wanted to have a look at the painting. Fortunately, this door was locked. I hadn't asked him to come and nor had Eddie.'

Giles looked thoughtful. 'Mm, I think I might have an idea who's behind that.'

Jess's eyes flashed. 'Not Lydia?'

Giles nodded. 'She was furious when she knew I'd given you the painting. But like I told her, it's still in the family, but of course, she's not happy with that.'

'Oh my God! I'll never be free of that bitch.'

Giles had nothing more to say on that score but he hoped for Jessica's sake that Lydia wouldn't continue to make her life difficult. He suddenly had an idea. 'I know a chap who works for Sotheby's, goes to my club. I'll get him to take a look, if you like? He can tell you how much it's worth and maybe suggest some restoration, if you're interested?'

'Thanks. He won't have to take it away, though, will he? Only I don't want to let it out of my sight.'

'It means that much to you?'

Jess nodded. 'I don't want the Wicked Witch getting her hands on it.' She was about to tell Giles about the whole Kate fiasco but thought it might bore him.

'Right, in that case, phone me when he gets here and let me speak to him. When he's been you might want to up the insurance.'

Jess looked blank.

'Don't tell me it's not insured?'

Jess lowered her gaze. 'I never gave it a thought.'

Eddie pushed open the door and came in with a pot of Earl Grey and a fruit scone and butter all beautifully presented on a tray. Jess knew exactly what was going through Giles's mind – like Charlotte's tearoom in Harrogate – but she didn't dare say in front of Eddie. That episode should stay safely locked in the past.

Giles poured his tea and added a drop of milk. 'Aren't you going to join me?'

Eddie, still feeling like a spare part, saw his chance to escape again. 'We'll be having our dinner shortly, but I could get us a cuppa, eh love?'

She nodded and turned to Giles. 'How's Laura settling in?'

Giles finished a mouthful of buttered scone and dabbed his mouth with the napkin. 'Mm, it's all been taken care of. Her shop's up and running, looks excellent I must say. She's very happy with it.'

Jess frowned. 'What's been taken care of?'

'The lease. I'm also handling her divorce.' Damn, he wasn't going to mention that.

Jess smiled and lifted her eyebrows.

'Ha, we'll see.' He topped up his cup. 'Excellent fare, by the way.'

Jess glowed.

Eddie came back with a pot of tea and two cups and started to pour.

Giles looked at him. 'And what do you do when Jessica's busy with the tearoom and the B&B?'

Eddie put on his proud face. 'I help. I cook the breakfasts and anything else that needs doing. I've also got me own little side-line.'

'Oh? What's that?'

He smiled at Jess and back at Giles. 'I restore and supply classic cars to the film industry. We had a company here in the village. I supplied three cars for the film. The premiere's coming up soon and I can't wait.'

'Yeah,' said Jess. 'I was an extra with Mandy and another friend up at the manor.'

'Oh? What's the film called?' asked Giles, although he had no intention of seeing it.

'The Manor House Murders,' said Jess. 'It's set in 1952 so we all had to look the part, and the cars.'

Eddie squeezed Jess's hand. 'We're getting married there next year.'

'Yes, congratulations by the way, Jessica's just told me.' He checked his watch again. 'Anyway, I won't keep you any longer…'

Jess stood up, 'You can have a quick look round if you like? Some of the rooms are occupied but….'

'…maybe another time.'

Jess's face fell. She wanted to show Giles what she'd done with her million and not frittered it away as he once thought she would. But deep down she knew he wouldn't have stayed any longer.

Before Giles called in on Laura he pulled into the village hall car park. He rang his friend James and asked him to meet him at the Park Hotel in Harrogate tomorrow evening. There was a painting that needed his expert eye, sooner rather than later.

\*

Lydia was still racking her brains. She had a distant memory of Giles having a friend at the yacht club who worked for an auction house somewhere in London. Yes! That might work. She would pop along to the club and grace them with her presence this evening and see if she could spot him.

She swanned in on a cloud of overpowering perfume, bracelets jangling. She quickly scanned the bar. It wasn't very busy, but she couldn't see him. The barman finished polishing a wine glass and came to serve her. 'Hello Lydia, long time no see.'

'Yes, just come back from France. Busy, busy, you know how it is.'

'What can I get you?'

'Do you know, Tom, I'm in the mood for a cocktail. A whisky sour, I think.'

'Got something to celebrate?'

Lydia smiled cagily. 'Ah, now that would be telling.' She scanned the bar again.

'Looking for someone?'

'Yes, I don't suppose you're expecting James tonight?'

The barman looked blank. 'James? James who?'

'Oh dear, I've forgotten his surname, tall man, Giles knows him, works for an auction house. Sotheby's I think.'

Tom screwed up his nose and scratched his head. 'Thorogood?'

'Ah, that's the one!'

'Can't tell you I'm afraid.' He handed her the drink. 'Enjoy!'

She took a sip, sucked in her cheeks at the tartness. 'I don't suppose you've got his business card to hand?'

Tom shrugged. 'Might have.' He began searching through the cards pinned behind the bar.

Lydia turned to see a man in a blazer, whisky in hand, sidling up to her. 'Hello, Lydia old girl. Good God, what brings you to these parts?'

'Dickie' Lydia looked around. 'On your own? I'm used to seeing you with Ron.'

'Ah, bit of sad news on that front I'm afraid. Poor chap passed away a few months back.' He patted his chest. 'Dodgy ticker.'

'Oh dear, sorry to hear that.' She gave the bar another cursory glance and sashayed across to the restaurant and poked her head round the door.

'Looking for Giles?' asked Dickie.

'Huh, don't make me laugh.'

'Who, then?'

'I was hoping to see James.'

Dickie shrugged. 'James? James who?'

'Don't play games with me, you know who I mean.'

'If it's Thorogood you're after, he's not around, old girl. Gone up north I believe, on some errand or other.'

Lydia looked as if she was about to explode. 'Damn and blast!'

'Problem?'

Lydia slammed her glass on the bar and flew out of the club.

Tom smiled and raised his eyebrows at Dickie. 'Something you said?'

# THIRTY TWO

James Thorogood knocked on the door of Bracken Farmhouse. Giles had filled him in on the details and he'd been in touch with Jess to arrange a time to value the painting by Edward Clarke on this Sunday afternoon. He had a vague recollection of this artist's work and he was eager to take a look at this painting. By all accounts it had been out of circulation for some time.

Jess had told Mandy and Janie that she'd be in the lounge if she was needed but they were more than capable now of looking after the tearoom and the children. She greeted James on the doorstep with a broad smile. 'Hi, not being funny but can I see some identification? It's just that I can't be too careful, you know?'

'Of course.' He took out his driving licence. She scanned it. 'Giles has told me all about the painting you want valued. I'm not surprised you're being careful.'

Jess handed back his licence. 'Right, come through.'

He wiped his feet and looked all around as Jess led the way to the lounge. 'Nice busy little place you've got here. I always fancied living in the Dales.'

'Thanks.' Jess entered the lounge and stood proudly to one side of Coverdale. 'This is it.'

James gave Eddie a nod and walked right up to the painting. Took out his spyglass and inspected the signature bottom right. Took out his phone and flicked through to find some other examples of Edward Clarke's work and his signature. 'Mind if I take a look at the back?'

'Sure.' At this point Jess remembered what Giles had told her. 'I just need to make a phone call.' She tapped her phone. 'Giles, it's me. James is here. You said to phone you.'

'Ah yes. Put him on, would you?'

Jess held the phone out to James. 'Giles wants a word.'

James continued to scan the canvas while he spoke. 'Giles.'

'Is it what we think it is?'

'Yes, it looks authentic, but I need to take a further look at the back.'

'And remember what I told you last night, about Lydia?'

'Yes, of course. I've got it all worked out.'

'Great! Thanks, I owe you one.'

James smiled smugly and handed the phone back to Jess. 'Mind if I take it down?'

Jess was feeling confident after that. 'No, go ahead.'

Eddie jumped up and helped James carefully lift the painting off the wall and lean it against the sofa. James bent down to scrutinise the back. 'Ah, yes. That's what I was looking for.' He stood up and turned to Jess. 'I'm pleased to tell you that you have an authentic Edward Clarke in your possession.'

Jess had never doubted it but she was pleased all the same. 'Awesome!'

'I gather you'd like to know how much it's worth, for insurance purposes.'

Jess nodded.

'I can give you a rough estimate today, but you would benefit from letting us having a closer look. If there's been any restoration or overpainting, it all affects the value. But you might like to know there's an exhibition label on the back,' he pointed to it.

Jess bent down to read it. '*Coverdale, Yorkshire. Oil on canvas. Edward Clarke R. A. Exhibited May 1930.* Oh wow! I hadn't noticed that before. What does the R. A. stand for?'

'It means he was a member of the Royal Academy.' He smiled at Jess and Eddie's bemused faces.

'Impressive,' said Eddie. 'So, how much is it worth, roughly?'

James tilted his head on one side. 'As a rough estimate, I'd say five-hundred.'

'Five-hundred pounds… Cool,' said Jess.

James smiled. 'No, five-hundred *thousand!*'

Jess's jaw dropped. 'Half a million! Oh my God!'

'That's well cool,' said Eddie. 'We know what to do if we fall on hard times, now then!' Jess shot him a look that said over my dead body. 'I am joking, love.'

'I can take it with me today, if you like,' said James, totally ignoring Eddie's remark. 'I can give you a receipt and a certificate of authenticity for insurance purposes.'

Jess tightened her lips. 'I'd rather you didn't. You see, there's a certain person who would love to get her hands on it and I can't take the risk.'

'Ah yes, I understand but our vaults are very secure and well-guarded I can assure you. Maybe in the future, if you feel you would like a more in-depth valuation or if you decide to have some sympathetic restoration work carried out? I would be only too pleased to help.'

'Cool,' said Jess, 'I never dreamt there was so much to it! All I know is that Edward Clarke was my great-great-grandfather and the sleeping figure under the tree is my great-great- grandmother Emma. They had an affair, and my great-grandfather Walter was their illegitimate son.'

James's eyebrows shot up. 'That's quite a story.'

'I know. Would you like to stay for a cup of tea in the conservatory?'

'There's nothing I'd like more.'

*

Lydia had sneaked back into the yacht club and found James Thorogood's business card sitting on the counter, snatched it up, locked it safely away in her handbag and hurried out before anyone noticed her. She had been planning and plotting ever since. This evening she poured a G&T, made herself comfortable and turned on her phone and her charm. 'James! Long time no see,' she said with a chuckle. 'How are you?'

This was no surprise. After what Giles had told him, James had been expecting her call and was well prepared for this conversation. 'Ah, hello Lydia. I'm fine thanks. To what do I owe this unexpected pleasure?'

A wicked smile spread across her face. 'You're too kind. I was hoping for your expert opinion on something.'

'Oh?'

'Yes, there's a painting you might be able to help me with. It's called Coverdale and it's by Edward Clarke. Am I right in thinking you've been asked to value it recently?'

He blew out a sigh, trying act as if the whole thing bored him. 'Correct.'

'Well?'

'Look Lydia, I'm sorry to disappoint you, but that painting, although charming, isn't worth the canvas it's painted on.'

'Huh, don't give me that!'

'No, it's a fake. The real Coverdale went missing years ago.'

'I know who's put you up to this! That painting is mine!'

'I don't doubt it but it's a copy.'

'How do I know you're telling the truth?'

'Why would I lie? There's nothing to be gained by it. Also, it would ruin my reputation and that of Sotheby's.'

Lydia thought about this. If that painting was worthless then the Blonde Tart was welcome to it. It was dark and depressing anyway. She would still like a second opinion, but she'd already used Mr Gambol and if he called at the Tart's residence again... No, she was certain Giles had put James up to this.

'Humph, I still don't believe you. I know you're in cahoots with Giles and that Blonde Bit. That painting belongs to me and I'm going to do my damnedest to get it back!' She slammed down the phone, her blood boiling.

James smiled to himself. He knew Coverdale was quite safe.

*

Laura hummed to herself as she got ready for her first day's trading. She put the last finishing touches to the window display and went outside to look. A little jolt of pride swelled in her chest and a smile played around her mouth. She'd stocked up with autumn and winter jackets, coats, waterproof trousers, boots and wellies, all in bright colours and cheerful designs. They looked great against the green and white backdrop of the interior and the gold sign above the window looked very professional. Yes! She'd done it! And it was all hers. Laura had glowed when Marjorie told her how very proud she was of her achievements. She knew Roger would disapprove, had she still been with him, and she felt smug knowing she could finally start living the life she wanted. Giles was being very helpful with the divorce. She had met him on a few occasions, here and in London, and it looked as though a relationship with him might become long term. But that was not something that was uppermost in her mind right now. First and foremost was to make her business a success.

The shiny bell above the door tinkled and in stepped a mother with two little girls.

'Hello, we'd like some wellies please. Have you got a children's section?'

'Yes, over here.' Laura showed them to a stand.

The twins' eyes lit up. 'Ooh, they're cool,' said Kirsty, pointing to a pair of yellow ones with butterflies on them.

Keira picked up some pink ones. 'I like these. Please mum?'

'Yes, all right. You'll need to try them on.' Mandy turned to Laura. 'It's a lovely shop. When did you open?'

'Today. In fact, you're my first customers!'

Mandy turned to the twins. 'We'll have to tell Auntie Jess. Eliot will need some wellies soon.'

Laura found the correct size wellies for the twins. They pushed their feet in and walked up and down the shop.

'Feel OK?' asked Mandy.

They nodded. 'Can we keep them on?' asked Kirsty.

'If you like.' Mandy started looking through a rack of waterproof jackets. She found a bright purple one and held it against herself, looking in the full-length mirror.

'Slip it on,' encouraged Laura.

Mandy zipped it up and put her hands in the pockets, turned this way and that. 'Yeah, I'll take it.' She paid for the two pairs of wellies and the jacket. 'I see you do men's as well?'

Laura nodded.

'Cool, we'll be back.'

'Thank you so much.' Laura watched them go with a big smile on her face.

Rudolf Pemberton-Jones had been lurking outside. He thought he ought to take an interest seeing as this shop was still in his possession. He was rather pleased with the rental agreement – it was helping to keep the wolf from the door – and he liked the fact that the shop was trading once more, albeit in a totally different capacity.

He had made the effort to get out of his PJs and spruce himself up in some green cord trousers and a sweatshirt that Rosemary had bought him three Christmases ago but had never worn. He stood tall, pushed the door to Rain or Shine and went to investigate the rack of wax jackets.

Carol shut the front door on the rented house she'd called home for the last thirty years, dropped the keys into the housing office and walked briskly down to the railway station. The removal men had been swift this morning and now all her furniture and possessions were on their way to the Dales. Mandy was over the moon that Carol wanted to move into the annexe and Kirsty and Keira were jumping up and down to have Grandma living next door.

The carriage was packed, and Carol was thankful to find a separate seat by the window facing forward. She'd never liked travelling backwards – it gave her an odd sensation and made her feel a bit queasy. It hadn't been such a wrench after all, leaving everything she'd known for most of her adult life. In fact, it had been life-affirming. There had been unbelievable changes in Peckham since she moved there as a young bride, some for the better, some not, and through it all she was thankful that her friends had always been there for her. Last night June and Sue had given her a little leaving party whilst reminiscing about the last forty years and they were all tearful when she eventually said goodbye. But Carol hoped they would make the journey to come and see her in the not-too-distant-future. She would miss them, of course, but living next door to her family would beat a solitary widow's life until she was carried out in a box.

Mandy and the twins met Carol from the station, the twins chattering excitedly the whole journey about their new school and their new friends. After their evening meal, Mandy, Trevor and the twins drove Carol to Jess and Eddie's where they welcomed her like a long-lost relation. 'Lovely to have you here,' said Jess and gave her a big hug.

There was a tap on the door and in walked Shelley complete with backpack. 'G'day! I don't suppose you've got a bed for the night?'

Jess threw her arms round her. She didn't dare ask how long Shelley was staying – she knew it wouldn't be long-term – but it was just amazing that she was there tonight, part of their big family gathering.

\*

Jess and Eddie drove to Harrogate in the Buick for the film premiere of The Manor House Murders. People stopped and stared as they travelled through the streets and Jess felt like a celebrity in the flash American car. When they reached the cinema Jess was a bit put-out that there was no red carpet and no paparazzi, but InPictures was only a small-fry company after all. Wanting to make the most of the occasion, Jess wore a long pale blue dress and white bolero and she had spruced Eddie up with a jacket and trousers instead of his usual jeans. As they sat in the centre of the auditorium Jess thought the film was surprisingly good, but she had hoped to see more of the party scene. She'd only caught a fleeting glimpse of the back of her head when the camera scanned the crowd. The part where Kate had interrupted had been cut, just as she'd expected. Jess wasn't sorry to see the back of Kate. Jess couldn't believe the lengths at which Cruella had been willing to go to, to ruin her, and to get Coverdale back. But Jess was still wary, even though Giles had told her that Lydia had given up on the painting and gone back to

France. The National Gallery had asked if they could have Coverdale on loan next year, but she still didn't want to let it out of her sight even though it was now insured.

Jess caught her mind wandering back to Bracken Farmhouse where Carol was babysitting with Shelley. She would've liked Mandy and Trevor to come tonight, and Ramona, but they hadn't been given complimentary tickets like Eddie. Eddie was bursting with pride to see his cars on screen – he couldn't stop smiling – and Jess was happy for him. The only niggle she had was that he intended to go in for this lark in a big way. She didn't want her precious land turned into a breakers' yard – she might have to have a fence erected to keep Eddie's business separate – but at least the approach road had finally been repaired. She still couldn't believe that Giles had pulled out all the stops and made the PJs cough up. She thought there was something he wasn't telling her on that score, but she was extremely thankful she hadn't had to find the money.

Trevor was getting a buzz from being property manager and making sure all the incomings and outgoings tallied. There hadn't been any more suspicious activity and Jess was confident that she wouldn't have to face any more nasty shocks where her finances were concerned. Mandy was enjoying herself in Jessica's Parlour, helping Janie on the busy days, and Jess was delighted that the three of them worked together like a well-oiled machine. It looked as though Janie and Darren would be literally tying the knot soon too in a pagan wedding on the moors. After the life she'd had, Jess hoped that this time round it would be happy-ever-after for Janie. Carol was willing to act as childminder while the tearoom was in full swing, and it was all working out perfectly.

The film came to an end and Eddie was well chuffed to see his name roll up on the credits. Jess squeezed his hand and kissed him. She was proud of him. There was a champagne reception afterwards in the foyer and Jess felt like Cinderella before the clock struck twelve. But this was different; she already had her prince, and her wedding was booked.